Advance Praise for One Icy Night

An Editor's Pick, and a "heart-stopping thriller..." **Booklife (Publishers Weekly)**

"It is thrilling, suspenseful, disturbing, witty and funny at times. You will not believe the ending!" – **E.S., Goodreads**

"One of my favorite thrillers to date!" – **K.C., Goodreads**

"One Icy Night is atmospheric, twisted, and a whole lot of fun, with well thought out characters who will feel like your best friends and worst enemies... Pepper took us through the storm, around some icy cliffs, and to the final breathless conclusion!" - **Kiersten Modglin, 1 Million+ Bestselling Thriller Author**

"W.A. Pepper's ability to lead readers through Rook's actual hell and back lends to a thriller replete with unexpected moments of enlightenment and revelation." – **D. Donovan, Senior Reviewer, Midwest Book Review**

"With its brisk pacing, engaging flashbacks, and a collection of well-crafted characters, *One Icy Night* is a commendable choice for fans of thrillers. Its appeal lies in the compelling combination of high-stakes scenarios, a strong female lead, and an addictive narrative rhythm. This novel is especially recommended for those who appre-

ciate stories with dynamic action scenes and complex protagonists."
(5-Star review, Gold Medal Winner) – Literary Titan Awards

One Icy Night

A Rook Thriller

W. A. Pepper

HUSTLE VALLEY PRESS
LLC

Hustle Valley Press, LLC

Print and eBook cover design by Damon Freeman and his team.

Formatted by W.A. Pepper.
Author photo by Taddy Pepper.

Danger's photo permission provided by his people.

Section heading images provided through DepositPhotos.com and provided by LeoNidkan, OkiePony, and StockSolutions.

Published by Taddy Pepper (Publisher) at Hustle Valley Press, LLC.

ISBN 978-1-958011-08-9 (Ebook)

ISBN 978-1-958011-09-6 (Paperback)

ISBN 978-1-958011-11-9 (Hardback)

ISBN for audiobook formats forthcoming.

LCCN Forthcoming

Professionally: The great thriller authors Riley Sager, Ruth Ware, Taylor Adams, and Rachel Hawkins, whose works and styles I love and have influenced my own.

Personally: To Dorothy, Gloria, Nan, Taddy, Tracy, and all of the strong women who have influenced and supported me in ways I could never repay. Thank you.

Thrillers by W.A. Pepper

- One Icy Night: A Rook Thriller

- DoGoodr (a Tanto Technothriller Prequel)

- You Will Know Vengeance: A Tanto Technothriller

- Running on Broken Bones: A Tanto Technothriller

- Burn It All Down: A Tanto Technothriller (available March 25, 2025)

Part One: Flurries

The National Weather Service defines flurries as an intermittent light snowfall of short duration (generally light snow showers) with no measurable accumulation (trace category).

Caution Level: Low

Chapter One

Ax

NOW

Through heavy, concrete-filled eyes, I study this madman that is trying to kill me.

Whether or not it is intentional remains to be seen, I think, as my brain buzzes along with the ringing in my ears.

"Snow don't act like this," says my whacked-out driver, Riley, who has consumed enough beer, tequila, and scripts to make Keith Richards balk.

The sleet hitting the windshield reminds me of *Star Wars'* Millennium Falcon going into hyperspace. Except *this* sleet is sticking like it is mixed with glue. The passenger windshield wiper sticks to the windshield before it snaps in two.

"It's like this weather has a mind of its own," he says, "and that mind is set on destroying everything it touches." He giggles at that. "It's God-like. I like it."

The wind smacks the side of the car, shoving us into the wrong lane of traffic. Riley overcompensates and yanks the wheel right and pain floods my head as the right side of my head bounces against the side window. Twice. At this point I'm so drunk, I either need to vomit, pass out, or keep drinking.

Instead, I try to speak.

"Shit!" I think I say that, but it could've been a thought. I try again.

"Look, I know you southern boys were raised on *The Dukes of Hazzard* and all," I slur in a jumble of nonsense, "but stop driving like you're being chased."

"You think?" Riley takes his eyes off the road and leans across the seat to look out the back window. "I bet you're right. They're always after me, always watching me."

"Who's they?" The words fall out of my dry mouth. Every word I utter tastes like cotton balls, sucking up all the saliva they can.

"They."

Well, *they* aren't going ninety-five miles per hour through this storm on a one-lane dirt road.

"Do you ever realize that every time you get behind the wheel of a car, you are a God?" Riley cackles. "You control the fate of each and every car, of each person, you pass."

"I'm sure that's exactly how they word it on the DMV exam."

Something between a laugh and growl creeps out of his throat.

"The trick is, each time, choose which type of God you are. Are you merciful..." He rocks the car side to side with quick little pulls on the steering wheel, sending me bouncing around in my seat. "Or are you vengeful?"

"Cut it out."

"Cut off the lights, you say?" He lets out a howl. "I like the way you think, girl!"

As darkness envelops our car's path, I punch him in the shoulder with everything I have.

"Ow! Quit that shit!" He flips back on the headlights and swerves around something I can't see. "See? We're fine. I'm just playing."

I would try to reason with him, but he's twice as drunk as I am, not to mention all the shit he's snorted in the last couple of hours.

A water bottle rolls across the floor and the itchy dryness in my throat burns. I grab for it, desperate for any relief.

"Don't drink that!"

Too late. I puke up my new companion's urine, adding to the smell of the world's worst tequila and beer to my ruined shoes.

And, of course, the smell and stains of the still-wet blood on them.

When I think about how the blood got there, it is enough to make me throw up again. I gag and dry heave for a minute before I shake the cobwebs from my head. I run my tongue along my sleeve like a cat grooming herself. My shirt isn't much cleaner, but I have to do something. If only my right eye would open, maybe it would help my unfocused and blurry left one. I want to put my head against the frozen-over window, just to feel the cold.

This asshole has his shitty vehicle's heat going full blast, so the windows are entirely fogged, and, despite his attempt to wipe a hole in the fog, I doubt he can see much through it.

I lean to the side, looking for something—anything—else to drink, but something holds me down. I fight the seatbelt. I yank and yank and yank, but I'm stuck.

No, I'm not stuck.

I'm tied down.

That's when I glance down and see the handcuffs holding the full-body seatbelt in.

Then I remember: those are the Sheriff's, who probably has just now figured out what I did to him.

If he ever sees me again, I'll go to jail for the rest of my life.

The roar of the defroster sounds like a pissed-off alley cat—more whirrs and screeches than warm and dry air.

The piece-of-shit car skids from side to side. With dirty fingernails, I pry open my right eye and the flash of an oncoming car's high-beamed headlights sear into my soul before I duck back down and cover both eyes.

"Shit! Ow!"

This-isn't-happening-this-isn't-happening. I'm-not-trapped-I'm-not-trapped-I'm-not-trapped.

Not again.

I claw at the release at the top of the oversized seatbelt. The latch and cuffs hold me tight.

"They designed the seatbelts for racing." Riley says this through chattering teeth. He's not cold. He's just on that many uppers.

"What are you racing in, Riley?" I snap. "The Pinewood Derby?"

He doesn't respond. Something through the small, defrosted hole in the windshield holds his attention.

"Whoa, shit! Hold on!" He yanks the wheel, and we spin on the icy road. Once. Twice. Three times. Hell, after a fourth-or-so circle I lose count. Then, like nothing happened, Riley keeps driving.

"These roads are no joke!"

I want to say that this car is a joke, or that his driving is. However, if it weren't for Riley, I might be in the local jail right now.

I've traded in detainment for possible death.

The world phases in and out. I blame the six—no, eight—shots of tequila and five beers I downed in the last, what, six hours? I'm more sober than I have any right to be; staring down the barrel of a gun sobers you up mighty quickly.

"You're kinda cute when you're not throwing up."

Prince Charming, everybody. Riley's still trying to get in my pants. Well, Mr. Driver, there's something in my front pocket, and you're not gonna like it if I have to use it.

He winks. The blood on his neck and shirt appears black in the limited moonlight. At least some of the blood is actually his.

The vehicle's defroster finally blasts air. Apparently, it only needed five minutes to warm up. As the oval-sized visibility hole melts away to give some view, I freeze. Through the sleet, in the distance, I barely make out something that shouldn't be in the middle of the road during a storm.

It's a man.

In what appears to be an orange jumpsuit, maybe prison issued.

Holding an ax.

And he's not getting out of the way.

Chapter Two

Callouses

THEN

As a traveling bassist in a shitty yet cheap cover band, you don't ask for much out of the joints you play. A decent stage. Good speakers. And a bathroom with a working light bulb that doesn't reek of too much piss and shit.

I'd confirmed the first two in *Stalin's Bar*. After glancing at the menu, you only get to *dine* here if you want a grilled cheese, a burger, or fries. The barkeep, a middle-aged burly guy who shares the same name as the bar, showed me around. He fits the stereotype of Southern Boy with his overalls over his light plaid shirt. There's a kindness and genuine concern that radiates from him. He's the white big brother I never wanted, I guess.

When I go to inspect the last on the list—the bathroom situation—I walk in on my boyfriend, balls-deep in my best friend's mouth.

"You've got to be shitting me!"

That line feels like the biggest cliché possible until my soon-to-be-ex-boyfriend tops it.

"Rook, it's not what it looks like." Cameron hunches over and zips up, catching the end of his cheating dick in his zipper. "Shit!"

"No?" I point at both of these pricks. "Then tell me what it actually <u>is</u>. Did Bekkahh get bitten by a snake and the only antidote comes from your cock? Or was her singing voice a little sore, and you offered to help it the only way you know how?"

At first, I think the strobing lights and red color of the room come from rage. Turns out the bathroom is filled with psychedelic stuff like a red lava lamp and trippy red lights.

"Now, Rook..." Bekkahh's off her knees and on her feet, wiping her lips with her forearm. "You and Cameron have been having issues."

"You've got a funny way of helping our relationship, Bekkahh."

Bekkahh shoves me, so I shove back.

"Jesus Christ!" Bekkahh screeches in a valley-girl pitch.

"Died for our sins." Stalin's voice precedes him into the bathroom. "Y'all good? I heard yelling."

"Peachy." I stomp out and head back into the empty bar. Well, mostly empty. Besides the four of us, there's an old yellow lab in the corner fast asleep on a beanbag chair. I reach into a cooler, and pop open a Coors. I hate beer, but I officially hate my bandmates more.

I should've known not to trust Cameron. He has more of a wandering eye than a kid at a candy store. As for Bekkahh, never trust anyone who spells their name like they're trying to win at Scrabble.

As I stand under a ceiling fan that only has one rotating blade, I hang my head. Our band is called *Mister Three Steps*, an homage to Lynyrd Skynyrd. Personally, I don't care for that band's music. Rather, I like it, not love it. The thing is, I hate like hell that they have the Confederate flag on the cover of their music. Maybe one day they'll wise up and put like, an American flag, on their covers or something.

I rest the icy beer can against my burning forehead. We were playing Starkville, Mississippi yesterday when we got the call that The Kracker Jacks, a regional band with a huge following, canceled their gig here. We hoped people would still come to the bar even if they weren't playing. In music, it's called filling-in. In life, it's called a bait-and-switch.

A metal tin sign over the bar reads *We Proudly Serve Schlitz Beer to Our Friends from North of the Mason Dixon Line.* From what my gambling uncle told me, Schlitz is shit, so it might be best that I do not tell anyone here I'm from Michigan.

My uncle is also why Gramma never had any money. Always bailing out his dumb ass.

The Coors' thick lager coats my throat as Cameron's hand caresses my shoulder. I don't even bother to recoil. He's not worth any reaction.

"Ru-Ru, look, you know that Bekkahh and I have a history."

"Don't call me Ru-Ru." I put my thumb over the beer can's hole, sealing in the liquid. "And I knew the history when I joined your dumb band." I shake the beer. "Just tell me this: did she go back to you only after we got together?"

Cameron sweeps his shoulder-length black hair out of his eyes and chews his thin lips. "Well, no, not really. You see, we had this *arrangement.*"

Friends with benefits.

I aim the beer directly into my ex's left eye and blast him.

"Ah!" Cameron claws at his eye as the sting of beer burns him a fraction of how much he's burned me. "You crazy bitch!"

This might be the best use of Coors Original ever.

"Leave him alone!"

Before I know it, Bekkahh is on my back. She's wanted to fight me since I took over vocals for that one show in Lexington, Kentucky when she was too drunk to stand, let alone sing.

The way she claws wildly suggests this is probably the dumb brunette's first scrap. However, it's far from my first rodeo. She's got my dreadlocks in one hand, but I've got leverage. I drop my right leg and right shoulder while flexing my left leg, and twist.

Gravity and inertia do the rest. Bekkahh crashes into the closest wooden table, breaking it on impact. A beer bottle flies off the table and smashes on the ground. I'll give this little five-foot nymph credit; she holds tight to my hair. We both slam onto the cold concrete floor. I roll up on her chest and pin her arms to the ground.

"Stay down." The truth is I'd rather beat the crap out of Cameron, but exes can't be choosers right now. My main goal is to stop the fight, not break Miss Blue Eyes' face. "Are you done?"

She nods, and I stand up.

That's when she grabs a sliver from the broken beer bottle and slashes upward. I hold out my left hand to block my face and the slash goes across my fingertips.

Time freezes. I barely hear the front door open and close as everyone from Stalin to Cameron to dumbass Bekkahh expects my hand to gush blood.

I glance at my hand, blow on my fingers, and dangle my barely torn digits in her face.

"Callouses, bitch."

You can't play bass without having thick skin, physically and mentally. In most quartets, you're always the last picked, even though you do the same job as the drummer, except with more notes and no stool.

Screw stopping this fight. I ball up my lightly sliced hand and bloody her formerly perfect nose.

"Damn, Rook!" yells Cameron.

As I stagger over and pick up my beer, I take a gulp.

A hand taps my shoulder.

"What the hell, now?" I ask as I turn after another full gulp, expecting the barkeep Stalin to throw my ass out in the sleeting rain.

Instead, I'm greeted by a white man with a full beard.

Wearing a Stetson hat.

With a gun on his belt.

And a badge on his chest.

Chapter Three

Waiting

NOW

"Look out!" I scream.

However, instead of looking ahead at the road like a rational human being, Riley looks at me as if I'm speaking Klingon or something. I grab the wheel and yank it right. The Suzuki Sidekick, AKA the Shitkicker, misses the man in the middle of the road. Our car spins in. Riley yanks the wheel back, sending us careening into a field with trees.

"Shit!" Riley turns the wheel back and forth in some mayday attempt to keep us from crashing. As the tree line gets closer, I brace my legs against the dash and grab the oh-shit handle above the door and brace for impact.

The sound of screeching metal is followed by a crush of tree branches over our windshield and a thud of wood slamming into our tires and undercarriage. We've crashed into a downed tree. Then, inertia overtakes our vehicle, and it rolls over the tree and into a field.

At first, I think I'm the one screaming like a gerbil in a blender. But no, the high-pitched yell comes from Riley. Everything in the vehicle bounces around and pelts us as gravity and momentum team up to beat our asses.

After three complete rotations, we land upright.

"Whoo! Yeah!" Riley punches the steering wheel and pumps both fists in the air. "Can't nothing kill me!"

Clearly, Riley forgot he just sounded like a four-year-old with a spider on his head.

What blows my mind is that none of the windows shattered. Not even the bottle of piss breaks.

What the hell? Is this car wrapped in bubble wrap?

My heart is a jackhammer, bouncing around in my chest and bashing everything it touches. My ears ring, and there's a sense of dizziness, either from the rollercoaster ride we just completed, or the casserole of tequila, beer, and who-knows-what-else in my system. Then again, it's probably all of the above.

Focus, Rook, focus.

I touch parts of my body, bracing for pain, as I search for anything broken. Luckily, I only wince at bruises, and don't scream because of shattered bones.

That's when I hear it. Popping. No. Cracking, like ice cubes in a glass of water.

Either oblivious to it or uncaring about it, Riley punches the accelerator. Tires spin.

"Huh?" He glances down at the floorboard as if the answer is there. "Why aren't we moving?"

Even though my body's stuck, my hands are free. I try to open the door, but something jams it. I can't quite see what's keeping the door closed. From the passenger window, I lean as much as my strapped-in ass can. That's when I discover the issue right below us, and I try not to freak the hell out.

"Riley, stop! Cut the engine!"

"Wait, why?" He guns the engine again.

"Because—"

The heat of the vehicle, coupled with the friction of the tires, breaks us through the pond's thin layer of ice. The car shifts to the left. Riley's head slams into the side window and Mister Tough Guy loses consciousness.

As we drop, I catch the glass bottle as it falls. Of all the things I might find as a tool, a bottle of piss was not on my list of must-haves.

As the water rises, I'll only have seconds to not screw this up. Unfortunately, that's not right now. Our salvation might require waiting.

Ironically, waiting has screwed me more often than not.

Chapter Four

Doomed

LAST YEAR

Sundays were always special to Gramma. No matter what type of fun I had on Saturday night, and no matter how sick or tired I was, Gramma expected—no, required—me to be up at six A.M. on Sunday morning. I'd put on my Sunday *best, which meant a floor-length dress with no cleavage and sleeves past the elbows. If you can imagine a black girl in Amish wear, you've got it. It's not that my Gramma was insanely conservative or anything. It's just what her mother made her wear, so that's what she expected me to wear.*

Sundays were also when Gramma put on her best girl. *This 27-piece wig by Sensational You gave Gramma's shaved head a Florence Ballard of The Supremes haircut: tight with just a touch of flowy black hair.*

She also brought her famous red hat. Only women of a certain age wore hats to church, and Gramma was proud to wear hers every Sunday. Wool in the winter and mesh in the summer. Gramma was of that certain age and then some. This looked like a UFO when it was on the counter. I think the brand was Scala or Scaler or something like that. It was bright red, and around the trim of this wool hat was a purple velvet rim about the width of a pencil. Then, around the middle of the hat was a band in the same color of purple. And, just on the left side of it was a fake apple blossom flower. Its white petals and yellow stamen or stalks in the center really popped against the red. Gramma was the talk of the town when she found this hat at a secondhand store. And when people asked her where she got it, she would just smile and answer with one word.

"Heaven."

Also, no matter the weather in Paradise Valley, Michigan, we'd walk to get breakfast six blocks away at a place renamed The Devil's Brunch. Once known as Club Three 666, this former nightclub from the 1940s at 666 East Adams Ave. was between St. Antoine and Hastings. It still had a two-inch-thick steel door with a sliding peephole so that the bouncer could look out for police. Inside, the aluminum walls reflected the scattered dim overhead bulbs. If drinking was your fancy, you could pull up a seat at the bar. It was a frosty glass counter that looked as if someone lined rows of glass bricks end-to-end to make it. And at ten A.M., a jazz quartet would emerge from behind a red velvet curtain and hit the stage.

Lifelong families of our area called this place Paradise Valley. Most first-generations called it Black Bottom. To everyone else, we were just an overpopulated part of Detroit. There was a rumor they'd move the Tigers near us because their ballpark was falling apart, but I'd believe that when I saw it. While I'd never been to a game there, it was a landmark that I doubted any Detroiter wanted to see abandoned. We'd already abandoned so much of this city and its history.

Gramma and I usually only got one or two jazz numbers under our belts as I ate a spicy chicken sandwich while she had an eggs benedict, extra runny. I said, "My, those sure look tasty," as a mimosa passed by me.

"Uh-hum..." Gramma didn't even raise her head to know what I was angling at. "And you look nineteen."

"I'm about to be twenty."

"And, wouldn't you know it, that still does not make you twenty-one."

"There are worse things out there." I stole a strawberry from her side of fruit and popped it into my mouth. "You've lied about your age."

"Yes, girl, lying about my age to get into World War II is the exact same thing as you lying to get some overpriced champagne and O.J."

I grumbled and went back to my food. For the next few minutes, we sat silently in the mostly packed restaurant. Gramma waited until we'd almost finished our food to quiz me.

"Sit-Rep, Lil Hoody..."

"Gramma, please just let me eat."

"Oh, am I inconveniencing you?" she asked as she pointed her yolk-covered fork at me. "Life doesn't work on your schedule. Sit-Rep."

Situational-Report: the act of knowing what is going on right now and how best to protect yourself. This is something, unfortunately, that most women either knowingly or unknowingly practice. Gramma learned it when she was a sixteen-year-old posing as an eighteen-year-old assistant to the chef for the 99ᵗʰ Flying Training Squadron, known as the Red Tails to most folks, or as the Tuskegee Airmen to history.

I put down my sandwich and turned my head.

"Nope." Gramma pointed her perfectly manicured pink nail at me. "If you have to look, you're already in trouble."

"I've done this a million times, Gramma."

"And all it takes is the one time you don't do it for everything to go butt up."

Butt up *was about as close to cursing as Gramma got.*

"Why are you so concerned all the time, even when things are going good?" I asked.

Gramma broke her gaze with me. I knew the answer before I asked. The way she overprepared me for life. Something happened to her. Something she never wanted to happen to me. She just wasn't ready to talk about it.

During World War II, Gramma was roommates with Amelia Jones and Beatrice Brown. Amelia worked under Colonel Davis, who commanded the Tuskegee Airmen, and Beatrice was the first black woman to reach the commission of Lieutenant. Though the girls rarely left the base, they had two rules: watch out for yourself and watch out for your sisters.

The truth is that, in any possibly threatening situation, you have under twenty seconds to know if you are safe. If you're a woman, those situations come up plenty.

And, if you're black, you'd better do it in half the time.

Gramma pointed two fingers at me, to mean I've got my eyes on you, *so I kept her gaze.*

"Six exits. Closest is twenty feet, but it will be the first one everyone runs to, so the second choice is the employee exit twenty-five feet away. There are twelve windowpanes that can be broken with a chair or blunt instrument."

"How many drunks are there?"

"Five, though two more dance partners are on their way to join the Tipsy Tango."

"Weapons?"

"All I can tell is that two men have boot knives. They are at my two and four o'clocks."

"And what weapons do you have?"

"My charm and my wit."

"Nope!" Gramma slammed her hand against the table so loud that I had to catch my coffee cup from crashing to the ground. "I know you're

just trying to be funny, but you can't think like that. The price of freedom, of safety, is eternal vigilance. There's no such thing as parttime *vigilance, Lil Hoody."*

"Jeez, Gramma, relax." I took a swig of coffee and answered her question. "Knife, fork, chair, car keys, and two glasses."

Gramma sat back, her lips pressed together, and her head nodded. "And there we go."

Then I mumbled, "Plus, my charm and my wit."

This brought out a deep laugh from Gramma. She was tiny, but her joy was immense.

After early brunch, we'd head to the Second Baptist church three streets over on Monroe. Just like her mother, Gramma attended here weekly. You didn't have to read the historic marker by the door to feel its history when you walked in the door. This church was the oldest African American one in the Midwest United States, and was built as a refuge for all. Founded by thirteen runaway slaves, it also became the city's first school for black children. There was even a historic section of the church. It was set up with newspaper articles, photos, and wanted posters for people like Harriet Tubman and fines for those that helped escaped slaves.

The church service itself was always powerful, even though I would sometimes drift off and dream of being anywhere else but in church. I was restless to keep moving, even in a holy place. However, when the service ended, we would make a beeline straight home and get in our jammies for our Sunday afternoon watch parties of two, maybe three, movies in a row—if my homework was done, of course. I got no say in what we watched, but there was a guarantee that Gramma was going to cut on some Charlie Pride on the record player and a Western film at one point.

This Sunday, Gramma put on a flick called Buck and the Preacher. *It was an early '70s Western not only starring a black cast but also directed by a black man. If memory served me, this was the first Western film directed by a black director. And that director was Sidney Poitier, who also starred in the film alongside my Gramma's not-so-secret crush, Harry Belafonte.*

I was under a wool blanket on the couch. It had a bad spring in the center that jammed into my back. Gramma was in her wool robe and under two blankets as well in her faded leather recliner. We were about forty minutes into the film when Gramma wiped her brow. I pulled my knees into my chest and steeled myself for whatever she was about to say.

"Whew, that Harry Belafonte, mm, he even sweats good!"

"Ew, Gramma!" I buried my head in my blanket as if Gramma was a monster under my bed. "I don't need to hear this again!"

"Lil Hoody, I'm just saying...I loved, loved, LOVED your grampa..."

It was always like Gramma to give a disclaimer before she said what really was on her mind.

"But give me twenty minutes with that man there, girl, and I'll die happy."

"I'm gonna go throw up now."

"Hush, child. Never forget I'm a human woman with human needs...and that...that's one fine human male right there that has EX-ACTLY what I need..."

"You can stop anytime."

"And I don't plan to."

We both laughed, but Gramma choked on something. Then she doubled over.

"Are you okay, Gramma?" I asked and left the couch to examine her closely. As she wheezed and sweat dripped down the left side of her head, I asked, "Did you take your shot, Gramma?"

"Um-hmm..." She pushed me away. "You're...you're ah, blocking the TV..."

Gramma had forgotten her insulin again. I headed to the fridge to grab the bottle. And that's when it happened. Her green eyes, the same color as mine, flashed wide. Gramma clutched her chest and recoiled in like someone just dropped a bowling ball on it. Her entire body attempted to squeeze into the tightest fetal position ever as she rolled from her chair to the floor with a thud.

"Gramma! Gramma!" I dropped to my knees as my grandmother inhaled sips of air, as if she was sucking them through an invisible straw. "I'm calling an ambulance!"

"No...that'll cost too much...I'm fine..."

I ignored her and darted to the rotary dial phone in the kitchen. After three swipes on the dial, the call to 911 went through.

"911, what is your emergency?" asked an even-keeled man's voice.

"Yes, help please! My grandmother is having a heart attack!"

"Okay. Please stay calm. What is your address?"

"We live at 233 on Charlottes, at the corner of Cass and Charlottes, across from the abandoned Charlotte Lounge." I spit all of that out quickly, and don't know why I was giving all this extra information to this guy. I doubt he cared we lived near the club that closed because Charlotte, the owner, killed her husband there and went on the run.

There was silence on the other end of the line. For a second, I thought the call had dropped. Then I heard what I thought was a sigh.

"Should I just drive her?" I asked, hoping that this would help the dispatcher help my Gramma get medical care faster. "We're only five blocks away from the closest hospital."

"Ma'am, you can do that if you like, but I can send an ambulance your way."

There was a click on the line. Had he hung up? Put the phone down? A feeling of helplessness filled my body. Everything from the hair on the top of my head to my toes went numb. The pounding of my heart hit my brain so hard it sounded like I was living in a nightclub.

"Ma'am," came the operator's voice finally, "we've dispatched an ambulance to your address."

"Oh, thank God. Thank you."

"Do you have a desired hospital?"

The question shocked me, and the dispatcher asked it so nonchalantly as if he were asking if I wanted a Coke or Pepsi.

"I don't care, just hurry please."

Gramma's breathing slowed and my stomach dropped.

"Ma'am, are you okay?"

"Me? Oh, I'm freaking grand…" I laughed—a wild, maniacal laugh. I was actually on the verge of freaking the hell out. Taking a deep breath, I tried again. "I'm fine. I'm fine. What should I do?"

"Just make her comfortable until the EMTs arrive. Would you like me to stay on the line with you?"

"No-no, I'm fine, I'm fine…"

I am so not fine.

Then, without thinking, I hung up the phone, dropped to my knees, and held my Gramma's hand. It felt extra cold, so I rubbed the right one until it got warmer, then switched to the left.

By the time the EMTs arrived, my legs were numb from kneeling. We waited for forty-seven minutes—for an ambulance to arrive to take us five blocks.

And that waiting doomed my grandmother.

Chapter Five

Hell Breaks Loose

NOW

Sit-Rep: The crash submerged the car in the hole in whatever lake or pond we just crashed into. I'm still stuck in this damn racing seatbelt, though the only race this Sidekick has ever won is first to the junkyard. Riley is unconscious, though he's on enough uppers and downers that he might wake up and pass out in the same breath. My only hope involves a glass bottle of piss that is slipping through my hand.

My rapid breathing isn't just from my nerves. Water is trickling in through the air conditioning vents. Even though I haven't touched water, the temperature inside this piece of shit is plummeting. I pull my boots up, even though staying dry is about as likely as this car floating out of the water.

Since we're stuck kinda sideways, Riley is closer to the bottom of the pond and I'm closer to the top. If I do get my seatbelt loose, I'll just crash into unconscious Riley. And he's irrational even when he's not whacked out of his mind.

I test a theory I already know in my gut won't work, but I must try. With my free hand, I dig into my pocket and take out the bottle opener I *borrowed* from Stalin's bar. Using my thumb, I flick out the spiral corkscrew, wrap my hand around it, and pound the tip into the side window. After six hits, nothing happens. Nothing more than scratches.

"Riley!" I'm not strong enough to break the side window with this small thing and mere strength alone. "Wake up!"

Nothing. Since he wasn't wearing a seatbelt when we crashed, his midsection slumps across the steering wheel. Thankfully, when the water rises, his head is level with mine. *I can't watch him if I'm trying to get us out.*

From the backseat, a gray bag that looks like a sleeping bag floats on the rising water. Using my foot, I shove the buoy into his chest. Like a sleeping baby finding his binky, Riley wraps his arms around the bag and floats. At least he's still alive.

Useless but alive.

The middle vent explodes. The pond and pressure replace the trickle of water with gushing water, covering my pants and freezing me. Twice I almost drop the bottle. If I do that, well, Riley and I both drown.

I try to flip open the blade part of the corkscrew, but it's stuck.

I touch the passenger window next me. It's colder than earlier tonight. We're almost there. All I need is a simple line of condensation to drip down the window. This is crucial. I read about it stuck in detention in the library reading *Scientific American* two years ago. It means the water pressure has reached a point where I can break the glass easier.

Two drops form, and excitement gets the better of me and I take my eyes off the air vent. Just like the middle console, water blasts from it. The force knocks the piss bottle from my left palm. As it falls, I catch it between my pointer and pinky fingertips.

If the bottle was empty, it might float. However, Riley's piss is gonna sink like a stone if I let go.

Now the water is coming in gushes. It covers my left side. It's freezing but I must stay focused. Soon, the water will cover my dreds, then my mouth. I look and see that condensation covers the passenger window. I angle my feet under the dangling bottle, say a prayer, and let go.

As it drops, I catch it between my boots. As the water gets to my nose, I swing my legs up and grab the bottle. With no time to lose, I hold the bottle with both hands and slam the bottom into the side window.

Nothing happens.

The bottom of the bottle is the sturdiest part. This should work.

It must.

I slam again.

Nothing.

Then. Something.

A crack starts in the center. The crackling of glass warms my freezing heart. The crack splinters out into a spiderweb. That spiderweb grows and grows until a cereal-bite-sized pebble pushes through.

The window shatters inward as water floods in. With that part of my bad plan accomplished, I drop the bottle and fumble to pop open the blade on the bottle opener.

It flicks open, and I jam the blade into the keyhole of the handcuffs. While this isn't the first time I've tried to break free from handcuffs, if I don't get it open, it will certainly be my last attempt.

Water covers my head. I'm a living ice cube at this point. My hands are so cold I can't feel the blade in my hand. I keep moving out of instinct, not sensation. Something in me tells me to stop, to let go.

Maybe being stuck in this car isn't that bad. All you've known is running. You can just *let go*, and everything ends.

A calmness sets in.

And I hate it.

Time keeps going. As my lungs burn, craving air, the lock pops loose.

As I surface for the little bit of air left in this piece-of-shit car, hell breaks loose when Riley awakens.

Chapter Six

B.O.B.

NOW

"Shit! Shit! What the hell?" Riley thrashes in the water that is almost to the roof. If it weren't for the bag under his arms, the water would've overtaken him. Now, it is as if someone set free a drunk baboon in this oversized Tupperware container called a Sidekick. Riley is pushing on the door, his door, that is clearly stuck against something. He even tries to crawl out the closed back doors.

I grab his arm. "Riley! Calm down!"

This does nothing as he pushes me away. I'm nothing but an obstacle to a madman. Maybe it's because I still had the open blade from the bottle opener in my hand. I am way too exhausted to drag him out, so I have one chance to convince him to get out of the vehicle.

"Hey Riley..." I keep my voice level before I turn it up an octave in fake fear. "*They* crashed us."

"They? Who's..." His eyes dart around the vehicle. "*They-they*? Shit. Shit!"

"Yeah, but if we swim out this window, they won't get us."

"Then move your ass, dammit!"

"Wait!" Riley fishes into his coat pocket and pulls out a gold pocket watch. He shoves it in his mouth, then crawls over me and takes the gray bag with him. I close up the corkscrew and put it in my front pocket. After a deep breath, I dunk my head under the icy water, and swim. Once outside the submerged vehicle, my head slams into something hard above me.

The frozen pond.

I run my hand along the ice, searching for the hole the car made. If it were daytime, maybe I could see it. I reach into my front pocket and pop open the bottle opener. As I jam the corkscrew into the ice, it has the same effect as when I tried to use it to break the Sidekick's window.

The cold is ingrained in my soul. I'm frozen. And drowning.

In the darkness, a hand grabs mine. I turn as Riley pulls me in the opposite direction.

Maybe he's found a way out. *I hope...*

We break the surface, gasping for air. As we shake and crawl our way to solid land, I plop down. My entire body trembles. My lungs equally suck in air and cry out in pain. Riley spits up his pocket watch onto the ground. He lifts my back off the ground and opens up his oversized camo bag. From it, he grabs a silver blanket.

"Wh-wh-what iz-iz-iz th-th-that?" My teeth chatter so hard I'm worried they'll chip.

"Sp-sp-space blanket, also doubles as sl-sl-sleeping bag, from-from my-my B.O.B."

Riley's words echo as if we are still underwater. The water must've clogged my ears. He sits next to me and covers us both with the blanket. It might be merely psychological, but the blanket warms me instantly.

"Who's Bob?"

"Bug Out Bag. B.O.B.," he says. At least, that's what I think he says. I'm mostly reading his bluish lips at this point. "It's full of In-Case-of-Emergency shit, and this, well, this qualifies."

If Riley has a space blanket in his bag, I can only imagine what else is in there.

"I think I have a soup in here that instantly heats up. Let me look..." He dives headfirst into his bag as the night air whips at my face.

I take a moment as something catches the corner of my eye. It's one of my dreads, yet it has much more weight to it. As I pull the ice-covered hair closer, it breaks off in my hand.

"Bummer..." *My hair is the least of my concerns.* "Your hair is breaking up."

"No worries." I fling the thumb-sized ice cube toward the hole in the pond. It bounces on the now-hardened surface. "I was due for a retwist."

"I think your hair is dope." Riley says this as he's digging through the bag, still in search of his miracle soup can.

"Thanks." Part of me really wants the word *dope* to disappear from the English language already.

A bit of warmth hits me and the pins-and-needles pain of my fingers getting circulation back hits me. I notice that I am still gripping the open corkscrew that I tried to use to break through the ice. As I angle it up in the moonlight, something behind us catches in its tiny reflection. All I can make out is an ax blade.

Still waterlogged, I never heard any footsteps, but someone had sure approached, as a hand grabs my shoulder from behind.

And, without thinking, I turn and stab as hard as I can.

Chapter Seven

Spunk

THEN

My heart dashes up the front of my body and strangles my throat. I can't breathe. The only thing I can hear, besides the roar of my thunderous chest, is some pop-country playing on the bar's jukebox.

"Am I interrupting something?" The white lawman's question is more of a statement than an inquiry. He unholsters his revolver and slides it down the bar. Stalin catches the gun and puts it in a wicker basket.

"Are you okay, little lady?" The lawman extends his hand to Bekkahh. I know how this looks to him, and I can't help but stare at the handcuffs and zip ties on his belt.

"I'm fine," says Bekkahh as she grabs ahold of the man's hand and stands. "My bandmate's just PMSing and has trouble controlling her temper."

"Oh, I'll show you temper—" The words escape as if they want to break more than that tramp's nose. I lower my head and put my throbbing knuckles on my beer can.

"Stalin, any particular reason you didn't stop this fight?"

"Damn right there is, Sheriff." The barkeep strolls over, tilts his head back, and shows the lawman a scar under his right ear. "I got this one trying to break up a fight between girls in junior high. You ever tried to stop two girls from scrapping? I'd rather step between a pair of coked-out Mike Tysons."

Without thinking about it, I take a swig of my beer. The cop sees me out of the corner of his eye, and my stomach drops.

"Stalin, did you check everyone's IDs?"

Shit.

Sit-Rep, Rook: You're nine steps from the front door, but the Sheriff is three from intercepting your path. Plus, that way requires fleeing on foot in the storm. It's out. My purse is five steps away in the opposite direction. Our van's keys are sixteen steps away and on the stage. The back door is fourteen steps from here, eight from the stage. There are nine chairs that you can knock over and use to slow a chase. However, once you get outside, you've got to sprint around the bar to get to the van. If the barkeep helps the sheriff, that's two pursuers.

I play it safe and grab my purse. Cameron grabs his ID from his wallet that is chained to his belt. Bekkahh reaches into her shirt, lifts a boob, and grabs her ID from under her bra.

From my wallet, I slide out my fake ID, spotting my real one underneath.

Which one do I give him? The sheriff watched me drink beer. But that's a misdemeanor. My fake ID says I'm twenty-four, but it's pretty shitty looking. Will work in a bar, but not with law enforcement. However, if he radios in my real name, he'll find out about the warrant.

"Miss, I'm waiting." As I extend my fake to the Sheriff, he yanks my wallet.

Shit...

He puts the wallet and the fake ID on the bottom of the stack.

As he examines my bandmates' IDs, I stumble through a half-hearted attempt to distract him. "Um, why'd you take your gun off?"

"State law," he says through gritted teeth as he holds Cameron's ID up to the light. "Can't carry and drink, so I've got to check all weapons with the establishment. Son, renew this before it expires next month."

"Yes, sir."

He takes a thumbnail and rubs the laminate on the next one. That's Bekkahh's. Mine is the one from Minnesota. It says I'm twenty-four. I figured if I was going to age myself up, five years would be more convincing than the two it would take for me to reach legal drinking age.

I'm just hoping that this white sheriff can't tell black folks' ages.

"Ninety-eight pounds, huh?" The lawman can't control his snick-er.

Bekkahh was probably ninety-eight pounds once. *When she was twelve.*

At least own that shit, girl.

"Being optimistic ain't a crime, I guess," I say, much louder than necessary.

A phone on the wall rings. Stalin picks up the receiver and says, "Hello? Yeah? Well, shit, alright. I'll let everyone know." He hangs up and says, "Roads are closing due to the storm, so no music tonight. Sorry, kids."

And to top off an already shitty night, now we're not getting paid. *Great.*

Just then, the smile that creeps across the sheriff's face is anything but kind. I totally forgot he is still checking IDs. "And now we have one Ms. Patricia Ann Craddock."

I hesitate because I forget my fake name for a second. "Yes, sir."

The sheriff flips open my wallet, and my stomach hits the cold floor. "Or is it Ruth Olivia Kellum I have before me?"

"Oh, that one's a joke." *Dammit, Rook, if you're gonna lie, lie convincingly.* "Actually, it's my cousin's. I'm, um, holding it for her."

As I hang my head I think, *Lord, please kill me now.*

He points the stack of IDs at Cameron. "Young man here called you something like *Ru-Ru*. Care to explain how you get *Ru-Ru* out of *Patricia Ann?*"

Dammit. The cop must've heard Cameron yell my name after I punched Bekkahh.

"It's a shitty nickname, but I prefer Rook."

"Huh." The sheriff rubs his beard and chuckles. "Stranger nicknames are out there, I guess." He keeps his head down and hands back everyone's ID.

Everyone's but mine. He hands me my wallet while he smiles at me and puts both of my IDs in his front shirt pocket.

"I'm off duty, so I'm going to wait to call these in until later."

Stalin chuckles, probably at the word *duty.* "Sheriff, why don't you just let it slide?"

The sheriff points at the bartender. "If you stand for nothing, you fall for everything."

Well, screw me.

"Hey, Rook, we're leaving. You coming with?" asks Cameron.

"You're kidding, right?" Bekkahh's contempt comes through her squeaky, dried-blood-filled nose. "She just beat my ass."

"About that..." The Sheriff points at the broken table, then back at me. "Do you want to press charges?

"Oh, come on..." Before I can defend myself further, the cop holds up his hand to shush me.

"No." Bekkahh looks me up and down. "Let trash be trash."

"Just, look, let's talk about this in the van."

Cameron grabs his guitar case and Bekkahh grabs her mic, but I keep staring at the sheriff's pocket.

Stalin leans across the bar. "Hey, dumbass, didn't you hear me say that the roads are closing?"

"*Closing* doesn't mean *closed*. We can get a motel or something. Ru-Ru, grab your shit and let's go."

Do I leave my IDs with him, or do I stay here and try to get it back?

If I leave, he could call it in. I see a radio on the sheriff's belt, and I'm keenly aware of his thumb dancing along the buttons. He might even already have our van's license plate. Also, with the roads closing, that limits the distance we can go before getting a motel.

I could go to sleep in a shitty motel bed and wake up to the po-po knocking on our doh-doh.

"I'm staying."

"You're what?" asks Cameron, his eyes narrowing in confusion.

"Look, you and that cheating whore can now stop screwing around behind my back because we're done." I put my finger on Cameron's sharp-pointed nose. "What am I saying? You're the cheating whore, and I never want to see you again."

"Ru-Ru, just calm down..."

There's something about the way this jackass says *calm down* that even the Sheriff feels compelled to speak up.

"Son, the lady says she's staying, so she's staying, understood?"

I'd rather stay with a cop who has my licenses than go with two fakes like you.

"Yes, sir." Cameron stomps around flustered, looking for his keys. "Where the hell are the keys?"

As I scrape this shit of a person from the shoe of my life, I can't help the smile creeping into my voice when I say, "On the stage, sixteen steps away from you."

He passes me, leaning in and whispering, "Thanks, freak."

Sullenly, Cameron grabs them and heads toward the door. He opens it, and a sheet of ice falls from above the doorframe and breaks into a thousand pieces on his head.

"Shit! Ow! Bekkahh, come on!"

As Bekkahh brushes past me, she stops and says, "Try not to kill anyone, okay?"

Bitch. I want to punch her face again, but I send her a shit-eating grin. "Eat a dick. Oh wait, you just did..."

"Girl Power and all that, right?" Bekkahh says with a grin to match my own.

"Right." I salute her with my middle finger. "Girl Power to you too."

As they head out the door, Stalin goes over to the jukebox. He unplugs it mid-song, then plugs it back in. The music stops, and he says, "Thank the Lord we can finally stop playing that Travis Tritt shit."

"Who put it on?" asks the sheriff as he goes behind the bar and pops open a bottled beer.

"That cheating whore," Stalin says with a wink for me. "The only country singer named Travis allowed in this bar is Randy. I can tell you where Travis Tritt can put his quarter: in the jukebox to play some Merle Damn Haggard, that's where."

"I hate pop country," I put in. No longer caring if the sheriff sees me drink or not, I snatch my beer from the table and take a pull. "I miss country where the lead singer just got dumped, and the dog got stolen, and mama's gonna shoot anyone who messes with her boy or her moonshine still."

"Yeah, mamas will do that." The sheriff takes a pull from his bottle as he scans my body. "Country music, huh? That's an...*interesting* music choice."

For a black girl. The words go unspoken but we all hear them anyways.

Normally, I wouldn't be bothered with such an obviously dumbass thing, but I'm too pissed at Cameron, Bekkahh, and the world to let it slide.

"I'm black, so I can't like country?"

Deliberately, the sheriff heel-to-toe walks over to me. "Sixteen steps to the keys, huh?" He nods at and raises his beer bottle to me. "You've got quite the gift for situational awareness."

It's not a compliment, but it's also not an insult. I take a moment before I clink the bottle. Somehow, I've got to get that ID from his pocket before I bum a ride out of here and regroup.

Then my white knight in a yellow raincoat enters the bar, pointing at himself and yelling.

"Hey, who has two thumbs and no inhibitions? This bastich!"

Chapter Eight

Run

NOW

The corkscrew jams about half an inch into the man's coat, right where his heart is located. I didn't think my stab would be that deep. Then again, I didn't think at all.

He's a twentyish white guy in a full one-piece red outfit. It looks like something a skier or bobsledder might wear, like in *Cool Runnings*, to stay warm. In his left hand, dangles that red ax. He's got the build to swing something like that and cause significant damage. He's about a foot taller than me. A set of ski goggles covers his eyes. A scowl covers his face.

"Oh, shit, I'm sorry, are you okay?" I'm staring at the corkscrew in his chest, so asking this question is about as rhetorical as it gets.

The man sighs and reaches a gloved hand to pull on the corkscrew, but it stays put.

"Damnation," he says, his southern accent so strong that it's more of a jumble of vowels than any actual word. He unzips his coat, yet the bottle opener stays attached.

The man yanks off one of his gloves and studies us. I can't see his eyes through the goggles, but I know he's studying us.

He points at Riley. "I know you, don't I?"

"I've just got one of those faces." Riley returns to his B.O.B. bag.

Riley had that one loaded to fire from the hip way too easily.

As the man shimmies his shoulder out of the red jumpsuit, I spot the good news. The corkscrew didn't break the skin.

It's quickly followed by the bad. He lowers his shoulder, revealing a pressed collared shirt under the red jumpsuit and layers of clothing that stopped the corkscrew's path.

Including a hunk of Mississippi-shaped metal with the words *Virtute et Armis* across the state and the words *Highway Patrol* at the top.

This is the last thing I expect.

So, I do what I'm good at.

I run.

Chapter Nine

Truth Won't Save Her

LAST YEAR

We arrived by ambulance and skipped any type of paperwork or check-in desk. The EMTs unloaded my grandmother on a gurney at the back of Harry Bennett Hospital and Rehabilitation Facility. It was the closest one to our home, and it was private. Of course, people told me that the main difference between a public and private hospital was that all its overhead lights worked. Once the vehicle's doors opened, the EMTs passed her off to two big male nurses in scrubs who shoved the cart through double doors and into a series of rooms where the temperature felt like negative ten degrees. The smell of antiseptic and cleaning supplies flooded my nostrils. The smell of the cheeseburger the desk nurse was eating alerted me that I was starving.

Harsh fluorescent lights forced me to squint as they wheeled my grandmother down a long white hallway. Everywhere I looked, people were hustling and bustling through the halls. They put Gramma in a large room with a dozen bed-sized slots separated by hanging curtains. Across the hall from them were private rooms. No idea how you get those. Nurses and doctors said things that sounded like English but were short abbreviations or medical terms I only vaguely recognized from catching snippets of medical TV shows. As a curtain on each side of the gurney separated Gramma and myself from other patients, I took a moment and examined the output on the monitor just above the bed. Her pulse showed fifty beats a minute, and her blood oxygenation was barely fifty percent.

I put my head in my hands. When I did that, I spotted something stuck under the tires of the heart monitoring machine. I crouched and pulled out a teal-colored woman's wallet with a gold clasp on the side where you'd keep change. There was a gold-zippered compartment that probably held a driver's license, cash, and other stuff.

As I stood up, I felt someone enter behind me. Startled, I shoved the wallet into the back pocket of my plaid PJs. I don't know why I did it.

"Hi there..." A redheaded nurse with a name tag that read Secretary: Lucy greeted me with a half-smile. In her arms were overflowing stacks of paper and clipboards that almost immediately dropped onto the white tile floor. "Well, phooey." I knelt with her to scoop up the spill: intake forms with patients' information, copies of insurance cards, and more.

As I combined my stack with hers, she said, "Thank you, my dear." The nurse's voice sounded more frustrated than appreciative. "I'm all butterfingers today and I'm running days behind on entering these forms. We do everything by hand here, so that all falls on me."

Our eyes met. My brain wasn't in a mood to placate anyone, so I just stared through her.

"Anywho..." Secretary: Lucy handed me a blank clipboard. I must've looked like she handed me something in Chinese because I just stared at it. "If you would kindly fill out your grandmother's information, we can start her paperwork. Do you happen to know where her insurance card is?"

"Yes, that I can do." My voice cracked like I was a crime fighter on TV saying I could solve the crime. I dove into Gramma's purse and pulled out her wallet.

When I handed Lucy the perforated card, the dead look on her face hit me like a bowling ball.

"Ah, well, is this her only insurance?"

And there it was. Gramma had Bandwagon Benefits, which was basically like not having insurance because it only covered the basics. Yearly physical. Basic prescription discount. Nothing earth shattering like an E.R. visit.

"Miss, this won't do. We are a private hospital and only accept certain insurance. Wait...does your grandmother have Medicaid or Medicare?"

Something stopped me when I opened my mouth. Just like how I couldn't order a mimosa, Gramma was four months shy of the Medicare age of sixty-five. Further, since Gramma still worked as a secretary at the factory, she was making too much money to qualify for Medicaid. I remember when I pointed this out to her, and she said she'd stop working the day the Good Lord was coming to take her home.

"I, um, can I have a minute?"

"Sure-sure, I can come back." However, before Lucy walked off, she asked, "Do you have anyone you can call?"

I don't think I even responded, because by the time I'd thought about it, Lucy was gone, out of the chute.

I stood there with my unconscious grandmother and all the weight of the world on my shoulders. Outside the chute, I was aware of patients, staff, doctors, and police that moved out there. Inside, I felt invisible. Powerless. Helpless.

Then the world crashed down on me. I fought back the tears as long as I could. I certainly didn't want to leave the chute, but if Gramma woke up, she'd see me lose my shit. However, I let the tears roll because all of that pain welling up in me needed somewhere to go.

The truth was that my grandmother was more helpless than me. The truth was that she was a working-class grandmother with one dependent who only brought home tip money from her shitty waitressing job between community college classes. The truth was she was just that in-between level of poor that's too much income to get government help, but not old enough to have them step in when she needed them.

That's when, deep down, in my gut, I knew the truth wouldn't save her, so I must.

Chapter Ten

Taps

NOW

I can't make out what he is saying, but I know the cop is yelling for me to stop running. Maybe he wants to help Riley and me get to safety. Maybe he knows there's a misunderstanding, and I didn't mean him any harm.

Of course, if I were a betting lady, I'd say there's also a chance he's thinking I'm scared because I just stabbed a cop.

That's not exactly why my feet are moving so fast that if I try to turn, I'll fall on the ice. I'm worried about the chance he's going to drag me to jail. Once they run my fingerprints, they will know who I really am.

And what I've done.

The sleet has picked back up, which sucks but works for me because that means the cop might stop his pursuit. As I hit the tree line, I dash past a jacked-up vehicle with monster-truck-like tires. It clearly is the trooper's.

Dive in, look for keys, and get out of here.

The thought occurs to me, however a better part of me says to keep my felonies at a minimum and keep running.

I keep one hand in front of me to block the small limbs from slicing my face. My frozen hair sways side to side, almost rhythmically. My dreads are now beating my face like it owes them money. Winded yet determined, I shift from sprint to jog, slipping every twenty yards or so on the icy ground.

After a minute, I spot a hollowed-out tree and crawl inside. As I do, I cover my mouth and stifle a scream as a family of squirrels shoots past me, clearly thinking I'm a predator. Once inside, I catch my breath.

Sit-Rep: I stabbed a cop. I have no car. No money. Not even my bass guitar anymore. I'm soaked to the bone and probably minutes from hypothermia. I need shelter that is more than this hole in a rotted tree.

That's when I see it: a trail with two ruts in it. They're not the deep kind, like you would find with a car or truck. They're narrower, but consistent.

A four-wheeler or golf cart made these. That means there's a house or cabin nearby.

At least that's what I tell myself. I gather my wits, breathe into my frozen hands, and then dash out.

I can barely follow the trail since this is sleet and rain, not snow. If a Michigan-level blizzard had hit Mississippi, then I'd be plowing through two to three feet of fresh powder. Instead, the trail leads me to a backwoods cabin.

The single-story building is pretty big for a cabin. Just from the looks of the old, logged structure, I'd say it is two, maybe three bedrooms. Before I examine the building, I study the area. There are no other cabins or dwellings. There is a red aluminum shed, possibly for tools or wood, seventeen steps from the back door. On the front of its door is a Master Lock. Since I'm not getting in there without the keys or a bolt cutter, I leave it alone.

There's a large flat area with ice covering it. Part of me wants to explore it, but a wiser part of my gut says to leave it alone. There's no ground cover on it, so maybe it's just dirt or maybe someone laid a concrete foundation to build another home. Besides these two structures, I'm all alone here.

At least, it looks that way.

I circle the building twice, searching for signs of life. There is no light on in any window. No noise from a TV show or radio. I also make sure there is no smoke coming from the chimney.

But there are tracks in the mud outside of the door. Also, the gravel on the side of the building is depressed, like a vehicle has been here.

Whoever was here, is gone now. I have to get warm and regroup.

I check all the windows. They are locked or frozen shut. I tap one of them and it gives a deep *pong* sound. Double-paned. I'd need a bat or bullet, maybe an ax, to break it. This doesn't matter because I have none of those things.

If only I could get into that toolshed, maybe I could get something to break this.

The front door is solid and has two side windows next to it. Even if I broke one, the grating is too close together for me to slip in.

That leaves the back door. I tap the glass. and hear a *Ping*.

It's thin. Or at least thin enough for me to break. I toss my elbow into the glass. At first, I think it shatters. Then I see all I've done is break the layer of ice on the window.

I prop my left arm against the door, swing back my right one, and smash through the glass.

I wonder if there is a security system, I ponder, much too late.In a panic, I yank my arm back and catch my forearm on the broken glass.

"Dammit. Ow. Shit. Ow."

In the moonlight, a river of black snakes out of my arm. I shimmy my shirt from my hand to the cut and tighten it. Then, not hearing any alarms, I take my left hand, lean in, and unlock the deadbolt.

Once inside, my shoes crunch on the broken glass. My instinct is to turn on a light, but I think better of it, just in case anyone *is* here after all.

That's why I'm going as slowly as possible. Deliberately, not desperately, searching.

The back door leads to a room with a round four-seat table and chairs. That is just half of the room. The other half is a kitchen. My arm keeps bleeding, so I go to the white sink. Grabbing the nearest dish towel, I wet it and put pressure on my arm.

Now I must check the rest of this place out first. I open each kitchen drawer until I find what I need: a flashlight.

Next to this kitchen/dining room is a living room. It's got a bearskin rug in the center of the room and a woodburning fireplace against a wall, but close to the center of the building. Next to the fireplace is a bookcase overflowing with hardbacks. There are so many crammed in there that when I grab one book to try to look at it in greater detail, the entire bookcase teeters my way.

Shit. Careful, Rook. The whole thing ought to be bolted to the wall.

I know I need to keep looking around, but I have to take a moment and catch my breath. My eyes skim along the book titles and authors as I catch the bookcase. I recognize some of the names of the authors, if not the books, as I push the case back against the wall. *The Firm* by John Grisham. *The Silence of the Lambs* by Thomas Harris. Others, I vaguely know or have no idea about. *Spandau Phoenix* by Greg Iles. Willie Morris' *Good Old Boy: A Delta Boyhood.* And a ton of others—I carefully step away.

Above the fireplace's mantle is the mounted head of the largest moose I've ever seen. Its cold, dark eyes follow me, as if to say *you are a stranger here, and you are not welcome.*

The mantle is dark oak, and there are two clay vases on each end. Each contains long-dead flowers that still hold their shape, and the vases are plain grayish-brown except for a single black streak in each one.

It shouldn't bother me, but someone unevenly distributed them on the mantle. Like something else was here and is gone now. I stand on the bricks in front of the fireplace and glance down, using the flashlight to figure out where my curiosity is taking me. I run my finger along the mantle, then look at what comes up. There's dust there, but not in the thin straight lines.

What was here?

Then it hits me: small picture frames would make these shapes.

As I glance around the room and shine the flashlight on the walls, I notice that the only things hanging, besides the giant moose head, are paintings. And, just like the mantle, there are obvious voids where a frame would go.

I walk up to one of the bare walls. As I run the light around them, the beam flickers.

The batteries are dying. *Figures.*

I smack the flashlight and the beam gets brighter.

Putting my hand against a bare wall, I run my finger along it until I find a lone nail in the center of the spot.

Why would someone remove all the pictures?

I let out a small laugh. *Maybe someone just hates their family photos?* I'm so tired and frozen that all I can think about is how pathetic I'm being in this pettiness. Me, on the run, after I just went through a hellacious night at a dive bar. Then I survived a car crash slash drowning just to stab a cop and wind up here.

I'm okay, I tell myself. I pick up something from a bowl nearby. It's a wire brush on a bone handle. In fact, there are at least ten of them in the bowl.

Weird.

Now that I'm sorta safe, I let my shoulders drop. I put my arms against the bare wall and stretch out my neck, then shoulders, and finally back and legs. My head taps against the bare wall twice, in both temporary relief and permanent frustration.

And then, from the other side of the wall, something taps back.

Chapter Eleven

Thomas

LAST YEAR

I don't know how much time passed. My heart and brain were in a struggle to see which could pound louder. A full body shake pulsed throughout my body. Either the rage building or the emotional drain of the day blurred my vision and caused me to cover my face and stifle a scream.

That's when a hand caressed mine. I lowered my hands and was greeted by a smile that would melt an iceberg.

"Picked a good day to cry, Rook," said Thomas, one of my old class-mates.

He towered over me since he was over six feet tall. His broad shoulders fit his T-shaped frame perfectly. Naturally, I'd had the biggest crush on him, but we'd drifted apart after high school graduation.

And this was how we reconnected: me, disheveled, crying, and as wonky as the wobbly wheel on a grocery cart.

"Oh, you know me..." I smiled and wiped away snot from my lips. "I only break down during good days."

"That's the spirit." He held open the chute and tilted his head. "How about some fresh air? We might not get much since there is the possibility of a storm coming in, so keep that in mind."

As we walked the corridors in silence, a sense of calm washed over me. Maybe it was just the thought of fresh air.

Or maybe it was Thomas.

The Detroit weather was oddly warm that day. It was one of those False Spring moments, where the winter's harsh cold took an early break. Nothing too warm, but not the cold that drilled directly into your bones.

"After this, do you want some coffee?" he asked, his long blond hair curling at his shoulders. "I mean, it's not good coffee, but it's available."

"Thomas, you had me at coffee."

As we stood in the corner of the cafeteria, Thomas told me what he was doing there. He'd taken to working weekends at the hospital since January because he wanted to be a nurse. The hospital always needed volunteers, so he served mostly as a runner. If a nurse needed supplies from another part of the hospital, Thomas was there in a jiffy. He didn't get to see much of the actual nursing, due to HIPAA and other medical laws, but he got to understand the vibe of the hospital.

Thomas also learned the ins and outs of medical care. I walked him through our whole situation, then he looked over his shoulder before he confirmed what I saw in the face of Secretary: Lucy.

"Rook, so to sum it up, your grandmother makes too much to be on Medicaid and isn't old enough to be on Medicare."

"Ding ding."

"And the insurance she does have isn't worth the paper it is printed on?"

"Hey, if you ever need an insurance that saves you ten cents a pill for acid reflux, Bandwagon has you covered."

I wanted to chuckle at my weak joke, but I didn't have it in me.

"Yes, we're in a pickle." I chuckled to myself and added, "when the boat's on fire, all you can do is put it out."

"Who sets a boat on fire?" asks Thomas.

"Oh, shut up."

He smiled and patted me on the back. I don't think it was this act of kindness that forced me to sit. I think it was that I'd lost what little steam I had.

However, when I sat down, something jammed me in the back.

"Shit. Ow." I reached into my waistband and pulled out the wallet I'd found when we first arrived.

"Hey, I've already paid for the coffee, so you're a little late there," quipped Thomas.

"No, I found this in the chute where they put Gramma." I popped open the gold metal clasp and flipped open the trifold wallet. In it was a driver's license, AARP card, a Diners Club Credit Card, and a sleeve for pictures. "It says the wallet belongs to Regina Leslie Tor. Do you know her?"

"Let me think." Thomas takes a swig of coffee. "We play poker every Wednesday. Let me tell you, she'll take all your paycheck if you let her."

I punch him on the shoulder, hard enough to mean something, but not hard enough to hurt. "A simple no would've worked."

"Do you have any idea how many people come in, wait, did you say Tor?"

"Unless I stuttered."

"Yeah." Thomas runs his hands through his long hair. "Yeah, I know her. And it gives me an idea. Let me check into something because it's a bad one, but it's something."

Chapter Twelve

Riley

THEN

The new guy is about four, maybe five years older than me. He's thin yet muscular, in a swimmer build kind of way. In the right light, his sharp cheekbones and deep-blue eyes might make him handsome. His buzz cut looks very military.

The stranger salutes with his ring finger down. The Shocker. *Classy.* He hangs his yellow raincoat on the closest hook. Then he sees me.

The sheriff keeps his eyes on the stranger while he adjusts his lone leather glove.

"Well, aren't you just a beautiful shot of coffee in our cream-filled world?"

And, just like that, this guy makes me want to throw up in my mouth.

I turn my back and grab a seat at the bar across from Stalin. This fails to deter the stranger. There's a certain rattle to him as he mounts the bar stool next to me.

"Hello there. I'm a good guy looking for a good girl. My name's Carl Riley, but you can call me Riley, as in I'd like you to *ride me.*" He extends his hand palm up. Just like me, he has callouses. Or are those burns? In any case, they are mostly around the palm of his hand.

Works with his hands. Maybe a mechanic or even a waiter.

I humor Riley and put my hand in his to shake it. Instead, he puts a way-too-wet kiss on my hand. As he rolls it over, he runs his finger along the scar on the inside of my wrist. I yank my hand away and wipe it on the back of my jeans.

"Riley, have any of your pickup lines ever worked?" asks Stalin as he cleans a glass with a towel and studies it in the dim light. *Clean* might be a stretch, as he never wet it.

Riley kicks his head back and smiles at me. I notice gold teeth in the back right corners. "Not yet, but I'm optimistic."

"The term is *repulsive*, Cooter."

Riley slams his fist down on the counter. "Man, you know I hate that nickname, Stalin!"

"Why do they call you Cooter?" I ask if for no other reason than to irritate him more.

"Because of nunya," answers Riley, baiting me.

"As in *nunya business*?"

"Uh, no." The joy and color leaves Riley's already pale face as he straightens up on the stool and rotates away from me. "Beer me, Battleship."

"Can or bottle?"

"Glass my ass."

Stalin slides the bottle down the bar, along with a corkscrew/bottle combo opener. However, instead of using the bottle opener, Riley puts the edge of the cap in the back of his teeth.

"Riley, don't—" The words barely leave the sheriff's mouth when a crunching sound like someone chewing on ice sends everyone's shoulders up to their ears. A look of panic crosses Riley's face as one of those gold teeth falls out. It bounces around the bar and Riley chases it all the way to the floor.

Just as he's about to grab this Mexican jumping bean, it slips through a crack in the floorboard.

"Shit."

Being the good Lil Christian I am, I grab the opener and pop the top for ole toothless.

A bead of sweat drips down his brow, and Riley takes a swig. The sting of the pilsner hitting that raw, exposed nerve hits him full force and sends Riley stomping around the room and cursing every obscenity I've ever heard of and two completely new to me.

Stalin laughs first, but we all ultimately join in.

Riley says, "Screw y'all, always making fun of me, because I'm about to be rich, and you're the one who's gonna pay me."

"Aren't you already rich?" Stalin says, preemptively laughing at his own joke. "I mean, you're practically bleeding gold all over my bar!"

The big guy's full body laugh gets to me more than the wit of his comeback.

"You'll see, Battleship, you'll see." Riley stares into his beer and grumbles.

"And on that fine piece of community theater, I'm out." The sheriff finishes his beer and puts down a two-dollar bill. Stalin hands over the basket with the sheriff's revolver in it.

He still has my IDs.

Sit-Rep: The sheriff is six steps away. His front pocket with my IDs in it is buttoned. That's a two-step move: one to unbutton, and two to swipe. Fall across his body and use my left hand to unbutton, then stumble backwards and catch the pocket with my right hand. Send his right foot back and left one in the air to do this right.

Go.

I take two steps toward the cop when he stops walking.

Then the sheriff taps his pocket.

"I haven't forgotten about you..."

Chapter Thirteen

No One Leaves

NOW

I jump back from the cabin's wall and almost fall over the couch. *What the hell was that?*

Maybe a limb slammed into the wall. However, that's an interior wall, so unless something crashed through the roof or in through a window, that's not a limb. Plus, if something had broken through, I surely would've heard it.

I tap on the wall again. Nothing responds. I enter the hallway, but don't see what could've made that sound.

My mind is playing tricks on me. I am exhausted, starving, half drunk, and half dead.

When my stomach growls so loud I think I've swallowed a pack of wolves, I turn my attention back to the kitchen. There, I find a fully stocked fridge. Some casserole in a CorningWare dish covered with foil. Deli meat that smells freshly cut, no slime on it or anything. Milk that won't expire for two weeks.

Sit-Rep: Whoever bought or cooked this is bound to return. There is a chance that they are not alone. I need to eat and get out of here ASAP.

I snatch the casserole and rummage through some drawers until I find a fork. I ease up the edge of the foil and move my food weapon under the top layer. This way, I can eat some of the bottom goodness without it appearing like any food is missing. Even so, I even out the food so that it doesn't look like any is missing. Of course, then the broken elephant in the room pops into my brain: the broken window.

One thing at a time, Rook.

Thank goodness I'm not a vegetarian because there's enough meat in here to make a whole animal. This homemade Italian lasagna has both ground beef and a slightly spicy sausage in here. It's good. No, it's great. The cheese-to-garlic ratio is at least six to one. That's one thing I'd heard about this part of the country: it is full of Italians that know how to cook a great damn meal. Before I know it, I've devoured two thirds of the lasagna.

So much for going undetected. I take two more big bites before I put the foil back on it tight and hide it in the back of the fridge.

Then, in the back of the fridge, I spot an old familiar frenemy: a 100 mL glass injection bottle. Even though I know it without reading it, I lean in and grab it.

Insulin, and it's down a few doses.

No one leaves the house without their insulin.

I would know.

Chapter Fourteen

Help It Grow

LAST YEAR

When we left the hospital cafeteria, Thomas got accosted by his supervisor and had to run some errands. I had to run to Gramma's apartment and grab all her medications so that the staff would know what she was on. I hadn't seen Secretary: Lucy in a bit, and I was hoping that maybe she'd return with good news. Maybe Bandwagon Benefits wasn't shit.

And maybe I'd grow wings and fly Gramma out of here. Back in the chute, I held a small bottle of insulin I grabbed from home. Somehow, I'd stared at the clear bottle with a basic black-and-white label long enough to inadvertently memorize every part.

Patient ID: 45233-AS5

Name: May G. Kellum

Insulin (Basal) Dose: (15 units)

Instructions: Take one dosage fifteen to twenty minutes after a meal, or when blood sugars need correction.

Expiration: 05/94

Refills: None

I can't tell you why the nurses only left the insulin bottle with me. Maybe because it was partially used. Maybe they were just overflowing with this expensive life-necessary liquid gold. I just didn't know.

The fluorescent overhead lights completely messed with my ability to tell time. I couldn't tell if it was four A.M. or P.M. The world was simultaneously standing still and spinning faster. All I knew was that nothing was helping my grandmother.

Gramma was never conscious for more than a few seconds at a time. The hospital was keeping her heavily sedated. Part of me thought they wanted to keep her chill until the cardiac expert arrived.

There were four waiting rooms on each floor of the hospital. I'd visited them all, continually walking to keep from thinking too much. The one closest to my Gramma's chute-room has ninety-six ceiling tiles. Eighteen chairs. Ten overhead sprinklers. Six sofas. And two on-duty desk nurses. The nurses in the northeast station were having relationship troubles. I could tell, because they were snapping at each other for the littlest things, like taking a pen from a desk. Or having put on the other's nametag on this morning, probably because they woke up together.

I walked the tile floors enough to know that around fifteen tiles per floor were cracked. I didn't count scuffs or scratches. What I was doing was maddening enough as it was.

The beverage machines were the kind you see on TV shows. There was no Pepsi or Coca-Cola. Nope. Across the front of the display was a red-and-blue soda can on a surfboard with the words "Surf Your Thirst" on it.

I guess that's how you market pop these days.

The food vending machines were also full of generic shit. Instead of Lay's Potato Chips, we had Let's. Mostest instead of Hostess. E&E's instead of M&M's.

I didn't even notice him until my stomach growled at the scent of pot roast. I turned, and Thomas held out a tray of food.

"Look, what they say about cafeteria food is true," he said as I took the tray. "However, with some salt and pepper, it'll be...edible."

"Wow, you're really selling it, Thomas."

I poked at the green beans that appeared to be more rubber than vegetable, Thomas withdrew a salt and pepper shaker combo from his front pocket.

"Say when."

As he sprinkled it on my food, I let him shake for ten seconds before responding. Then, after a forkful of shoe-leather-tough pot roast, I chewed for a good minute before it went down.

"Better?"

"Define better..."

I carried the tray and we walked the halls. As we got close to Gramma's chute, I pointed my fork at the private rooms across the hall.

"So, besides a private room, what else does good insurance get you?" I asked.

"Ah, that's what I wanted to run by you." Thomas snatched the fork from my hand, stabbed a green bean, put it in his mouth, then spit it in the trash. "Do you still have that wallet?"

"Damn, I pawned it five minutes ago; of course I still have it." I yanked the fork back and grabbed another bit of barely edible food.

"Walk with me." His tone was kind, yet stern.

As we strolled past the closed doors that all had white boards with multiple colors of ink on them, a patient's first and last name, followed by a date of birth, was in the center of the board. On the side of the boards were initials from nurses and times, probably when the patient was last checked on. Finally, written on the white boards were various abbreviations. "What do these mean? AA? Someone that shouldn't be allowed near an open bar?"

Thomas rubbed his chin before he spoke. "That's Acute Appendectomy. This particular patient is recovering from surgery."

"Acute means unwelcome," I mumbled through a mouthful of food. "Who actually has a welcomed Appendectomy?"

"Don't try to make sense of medicine," Thomas said with a chuckle. "You'll just drive yourself mad."

As I pointed to each sign on our stroll, Thomas walked me through the terms. A light would twinkle in his eyes as he talked about whatever the abbreviations made him think about. When we got to the last one, right next to the elevator, as opposed to the white board having black ink on it, it had red.

"This is what I wanted to tell you about."

As I studied the board, I asked, "Why is it red?"

"Most people don't catch that..." Thomas looked over both of his shoulders before he continued. "Red means someone is on an end-of-life regime. The M.S. means morphine sulfate. Our patient here, one Miss Regina Tor, is finishing her battle with cancer on her own terms."

"Huh...," I said as our eyes met. "So, she's not going home to die around family?"

"Nope. No family. Just dying slowly and nearly anonymously. And with really good insurance."

Thomas had planted a seed. Now it was up to me to decide whether to help it grow.

Chapter Fifteen

That Noise

NOW

Now that my body is acting rationally, like showing signs of hunger and fatigue, my bladder reminds me of all the poor decisions I made tonight. The massive amounts of tequila and beer I consumed demand freedom.

Sit-Rep: If I don't pee, I explode.

As the pressure in my midsection builds, I pass by the living room and enter a long hallway. I check the first door on my right. It opens to an attached garage, complete with boxes, things covered with tarps, and a dust-covered Volkswagen Bug straight out of a Herbie movie.

Even though it is old, it still might crank.

Back in the hallway, I check the door directly in front of me. A bathroom complete with a tub/shower combo welcomes me as if it had a neon sign *Relief Is Here*. Since there are no outside windows in here for anyone to see in, I turn on the light. The moment my eyes spot the porcelain, it is an all-out race. Once I plop down, the relief overtakes my body.

As a waterfall explodes between my legs, I rest my head in my hands. It's not because of this epic piss. Well, it helps. No, it is that I finally have a moment to think about how screwed I really am.

Sit-Rep: I have no money, though I might find some in this house. So far, all I've done is break-and-enter, not steal anything. Well, some lasagna, and that's worth whatever fine they give me. Right now, I'm trespassing. If I am going to steal the car, that's grand theft auto; I might as well steal some cash as well.

Damn, how'd it come to this?

No sooner have I flushed the toilet than I hear it: the sound of a door closing.

Shit!

I cut off the bathroom light and pull up my pants. The water pipe that connects to the toilet hisses, probably because of temperature dropping and freezing pipes. I drop to my knees and fumble in the dark to find the knob to stop the incoming water to the toilet. Anything to stop noises. I turn the knob. A glurg of water slips between the grooves and soaks my hand. After four turns, the hiss quiets like a balloon running out of air.

I glance at the bathroom door.

It was closed when I got here, right? Wait, was it barely open, or completely shut? Shit. Shit! I wasn't even really looking at it. I just walked in. Think, Rook, think.

I crawl along the floor and turn the doorknob just enough to open the door a crack. Then my wet hand slips and the lock pops back against the frame.

Shit!

Foot stomps get louder. I dart into the tub and shower combo, pull the curtain, and crouch as low as possible.

Dammit! I've left my flashlight on the floor near the toilet. I sneak my hand out of the curtain and stretch as far as possible.

I grab it and clutch the lens to my chest as the door flings open. The overhead bathroom light blinds me. I lay like a corpse in the tub. The warmness of my flashlight's bulb pressed against my chest burns slightly. Yet I don't dare click the light off or move the beam from me.

In the background, I hear something rhythmic, but I can't quite place it. A few seconds pass until the steps approach the tub. The shadow looks like a man.

If he leans down to open the tub, I can clock him with the flashlight. It won't knock him out, but maybe I can run.

Unless the person gets on top of me in the tub or I get stuck in the curtain like in some Friday the 13th movie. I have no room to fight or kick.

The sound of a zipper precedes a piss.

He's not too broad, but he has me at a disadvantage because I'm stuck in a damn bathtub.

The rhythmic sound continues and strain my ears to place the sound. Then it hits me:

I know that exact ticking sound.

"Riley?"

"Shit!" He stumbles back and zips up like I'm his mom and I just caught him playing with his johnson. He's looking around the room for whoever said that. His silhouette looks at the ceiling. "Jesus?"

I pull the curtain and say, "Our Lord and Savior."

Riley screams and falls back. "What the hell are you doing in the tub?"

"Oh, you know me, I'm a hardcore fan of old-school porcelain and this tub is from the early 1800s."

His eyebrows raise. "So, it's valuable?"

"No, you idiot, I'm hiding."

He extends his hand to me. Even though I'm pretty sure it's the one he used to hold his prick, I grab it with both hands as he pulls me up. "What are you doing here?"

"Me?" He shrugs, and I notice a little bit of swelling and blood on his bottom lip. "I live here. Also, how'd you know it was me?"

I tap his front pocket. He withdraws the gold pocket watch.

"Ah." He puts it back in and says, "I looked all over for you. Why'd you run off?"

Because I'm wanted by the law and just lightly stabbed a highway patrolman.

"I think I hit my head in the crash and wasn't thinking straight." I rub my scalp to help sell the story. "So, what happened after I left?"

"Oh, you know, he's gonna file a report for my car in the morning. The guy was clearing the road when we saw him. He didn't take any offense to your ruining his jumpsuit, by the way."

"Well, that's good."

Riley is still all wet, but his clothes look more tattered than I remember. There are tears. Maybe he got them caught on the same limbs that ripped up my hand as I ran. That could also explain that busted lower lip. Still, something feels off. It's like when you drink milk that says *expired* on the carton, but smells okay, so you drink it anyway.

"What is the officer's name?"

"Patrolman." A smartass smile crosses Riley's face as his eyes roll left. "Bobby Howler."

Okay. He said that name pretty quickly. Maybe he's telling the truth.

As we leave the bathroom, Riley stops in the hallway, halting our progress.

"Everything okay?" I ask. "I know I stopped your pissing, so if you need some privacy..."

"Did you go into the shed or any other rooms?" Riley's back is to me, though he tilts his right ear my way.

"Just the kitchen and garage."

"Good. Good." Riley clearly senses I'm about to ask *why*, so he heads off my unasked question. "There's a room where the floorboards have rotted away, so don't go in there unless you want to fall through."

It's like one of those 3D pictures that look like one thing until you let your eyes go out of focus. At one point, you should see another picture.

There's something about Riley I can't see yet.

Like why there are no pictures on the wall, and why he has a nice gold watch.

"Which room is that?"

Even though he points, in my gut I know the answer.

It is the one on the other side of where I heard that noise.

Chapter Sixteen

BAND-AID on a Gushing Wound

LAST YEAR

If I was going to forge this insurance, the first thing I needed to do was find a copier that no one was using. It would also help if there weren't prying eyes on me. That's why I left the hospital and went to the hotel attached to it. Once inside, I found a copier, computer, and even office supplies in the business center. Unfortunately, the business center was locked and only an active hotel key card would open it.

I headed to the front desk, my shoes thwapping against the marble tile. There a guy greeted me with dead eyes and a shit-eating grin.

"Welcome to the HB Hotel. How may I assist you?"

On the desk were what you expected: a sign-in sheet, a pen anchored with a chain to the desk, and a bowl with returned hotel room key cards. Next to the bowl was a sign that read all keys are automatically reset on the day of checkout at ten A.M. *I checked my watch: 11:32. I'd thought about stealing one from the bowl, but a card from the pile wouldn't work.*

"Yes, I was wondering if you could point me to your business center, please," I said with a glance over the sign in sheet.

"Miss, only hotel guests may use the business center."

"Well, I'm staying here."

"Really?" His raised eyebrow and snicker made me want to punch him in his very punchable face. "What name and room number?"

"Sampson, Lyle."

At least that's what the most legible signature looked like. *Maybe he'll think I'm Lyle's kid.*

When the clerk moved his attention from me to the computer on his side of the desk, I snuck my hand into the bowl of returned key cards and snagged several. From behind me, I heard footsteps stop.

A line just formed. That might help me.

"And room number?"

"Can't say." This bit of truth caught Mister Punchable off-guard. There was no way for me to know the room number because it wasn't listed on the sheet. As I shuffled the key cards in my hands, I was hoping to find anything that worked.

I turned to look over my shoulder as the sound of bags hitting the floor echoed in the room. Now there were three people in line. All looked agitated.

"Without a room number, I'm sorry. I can't give you access to the business center. I'm going to have to ask you to leave."

I looked at the line. It had grown to five worn-out-looking business-men and -women. All looked tired and a little annoyed with me. Which was absolutely perfect for what came next.

I rubbed my right eye and sighed as I put my head on the front desk. "Look, it was late, and Mom and Dad were fighting when we got here *last night. I slept in the bathtub because they were yelling and yelling, and none of this would've have happened if Dad hadn't slept with his secretary." I propped my head up and increased my volume. Not enough to get thrown out, but enough to get more attention. "It wasn't the first time, and, in Dad's defense, Mom cheated first with someone who works at this very hotel."*

"Um, miss..." The clerk's eyes went wide. He attempted to shush me as if I was a child.

That's when I got twice as loud.

"Granted, this started like, almost twenty years ago." I jerked back like a bee just flew in my face. "Wait! I'm almost twenty! What if one of your employees is my real dad?"

"Miss, please, you're causing a scene."

I swayed side to side as he leaned forward and added the two words that were his kiss of death.

"Calm down."

"Don't tell me to calm down!*"*

This dumbass just pulled the starter pistol's trigger for the Difficult Woman Race, *and I had my track shoes on.*

"Don't do it! Look, my father is one of your employees, and I want to meet him! I demand it!"

As sweat trickled down the man's straight black hair and got into his eyes, he made his choice. In under five seconds, the clerk coded a key card and handed it to me.

"Have a nice day, ma'am."

Go big or stay home.

As I snatched the card, I mouthed the words thank you, but kept acting like I was about to burst into tears.

Before I got two steps, a hand was on my shoulder.

"*I hope everything works out with your dad,*" said a nice redheaded lady.

I nodded and went to the business center. There was one Mac in the corner and a basic brownish typewriter next to it. First, I raided the business supplies. Then I found a bottle of Wite-Out, Scotch tape, and scissors. I made a color photocopy of Miss Regina's insurance card. Next, I took the Wite-Out and removed her name. On this whited-out version, I made another copy. That's when I put the page into the typewriter and typed Gramma's name in.

Finally, I made one final copy, and cut it to fit the normal size.

The copy was grainy, but it should work.

Might work.

Please work.

Then I took the red paper I stole from the nurse's station and made a copy of the fake insurance card on the paper. If I dropped it into that stack on the desk, Gramma might get the treatment she deserves.

This was a BAND-AID on a gushing wound, but I had to try. Whatever the fallout, I'd burn that bridge when I got to it.

Chapter Seventeen

Mother Nature

NOW

Riley and I enter the living room. There, on the checkered cloth couch, is Riley's camo B.O.B., as he calls it.

"We need some tools to cover up that hole you made." Riley's tone is joyful, almost like he is excited to repair the window I broke. "There's a shed outside that has what we need."

"I tried it earlier, but it's locked."

Riley dangles a keychain with a small pink elephant on it. "I'll go grab what we need if you gather some firewood because, unfortunately, the fireplace is wood-burning."

"Is the cabin's heat gas or electric?"

"Gas, but the thermostats are electric, so if the power goes out, the point's moot." The wind whips at the windows, and they creak as if they're predicting how bad the storm will get. "You want some cocoa before or after you head out?"

Sit-Rep: Something is off about Riley. He's hiding something. Correction, he's hiding several things. For example, he doesn't seem the type to have a pink elephant keychain. If I get wood now, I can think of questions to ask him when I get back, then pivot accordingly. If I get cocoa now, I can decide if I use that time gathering wood to actually get the hell out of here.

"The cocoa will warm me up afterward."

Riley walks to the front door and opens a side closet next to it. From inside, he grabs a long white winter coat and tosses it to me. When I put it on, I notice the pink lining.

"This doesn't seem like your cup of tea, Riley."

"It's my grandma's." He points around the cabin. "This is—*was* her place."

"Oh, I'm so sorry."

Riley clicks his tongue and says, "Don't be. She's in a better place."
I never took Riley for the religious type.

He leans in and grabs a set of sturdy flashlights. Instead of tossing me one, he hands the black billy-club-looking thing to me.

"Watch out for the frozen pond in the backyard. It's about a hundred yards south-southeast."

That's the area my gut told me to stay clear of. Falling into one body of water tonight is more than enough for me.

"Thanks for the heads-up."

"If you run across a weird-looking manhole cover in the ground, you've gone too far."

"What's that, a sewer?"

"Ha!" Riley shakes his head. "Everything is septic out in this county. No, that's a tornado shelter. Built sturdy and deep. If we need additional food, water, or medical supplies, they're in there."

"Are there lots of tornadoes here?"

"Not a lot, but it only takes one to take everything," he says with a shit-eating grin. "Also, it's easy to get lost out there, even with decent visibility. There's not another home for about six klicks."

Instead of asking *what the hell is a klick?* I shrug.

"Military distance." He holds up his fingers and stretches the distance between them. "It's the same as a kilometer."

"Then why didn't you just say that?"

"Because I'm trying to impress you."

I don't know yet how, but it might help to play along.

"I'll let you know when that's working," I say with a smile.

Riley opens the door. Icy wind smacks us both in the face. While I instinctively duck my head, Riley takes the blast straight on.

"Yeah, this ain't gonna be pretty." He leans out and grabs something next to the door. I can't quite see what it is until he puts it in front of me. It's an ax with a wooden handle. It looks quite worn, as the red blade has large nicks and gashes in the side.

It also looks a lot like the ax that highway patrolman had.

He extends it to me. "You probably won't need this, but just in case." Without thinking, I instinctively grab the handle and step through the door.

The rain and sleet mixture pelts my face as I pull the hood over my head. The sky is a weird mixture of patchy auras, with weird light dancing high above me in the icy clouds. I don't know if it is this storm cell or the cloud cover trying to let the moonlight in.

I turn to head to the trees to my right when a hand grabs my arm.

"Wait..." Riley reaches into his pockets and hands me brown work gloves. "Ax work will tear your hands up. Plus, these will keep you warm."

As I raise an eyebrow, I ask "Won't your hands freeze out here?"

He smiles and dances his digits in front of my face. "I'm going to have to use my hands to warm the lock on the shed. In these temperatures, turning a lock without warming it could break or chip the tumblers, so a little frigidness is better than a broken lock."

Not as dumb as he pretends to be. Noted.

"Good to know." The warmth of Riley's gloves steels me. "You ready?"

"If you're feeling froggy, then jump."

I take that as *yes,* and head out.

The stomp of crunchy ground, ice-covered grass, under my feet almost echoes in this nighttime oblivion. I make it about fifty yards before I find some downed trees. The trees aren't rotten, nor did they get struck by lightning, because I find no scorch marks on the split wood. They've simply fallen from the weight of the ice. With ax in hand, I step back, plant my feet, and heave the ax over my head. The *thunk* of the blade lands not in wood, but in solid ice. I pull on the ax. Nothing.

"Dammit."

I plant my foot on the log and pull with all my weight. The next thing I know, I'm on my back holding a wooden handle. As the rainy sleet pelts my face, I sigh.

"Shit."

I crawl up to the log and see what I already know is true: the red ax head is stuck in the ice slash log.

"Of course."

I take the ax handle, place it under the blade, and create a fulcrum. It takes four good pushes and a lot of profanity before the ax head pops loose. When it does, it takes a chunk of something with it.

I pick up both the ax head and the chunk of ice. The blade is fine, but so is the chunk of ice. It's a good three inches thick.

As I examine the limbs of the trees, even the smallest of branches has a good two to three inches of ice wrapping it.

Is this much ice covering everything it lands on?

It is at this moment that I notice how many trees cover us. I'd gone to the woods to gather firewood, but the cabin itself has over a dozen, no, two dozen giant trees surrounding it. There are tree branches the length of city buses that extend over the house.

How long before this Act of God works with Mother Nature and crashes it all down on us?

Chapter Eighteen

My Moral Code

LAST YEAR

Once I had a decent enough fake insurance card, I ran all over that hospital. Somewhere I'd find Secretary: Lucy. And, as luck would have it, she was a floor above our ER chute.

In true Lucy fashion, her arms were overflowing with paper and clipboards. I guess she didn't even recognize me at first because she said, "Oh, I'm not an attending nurse."

"No, I know that." I reached into my back pockets and pulled out Gramma's insurance card. "I looked through Gramma's purse again. I was so scattered that I didn't check the very bottom. You know, the part with unwrapped peppermints and random tops to mascara?"

Secretary: Lucy laughed. "Don't I know it."

"So, I wonder would this help?" I asked as I were asking a basic question to a child.

Lucy adjusted her glasses and smiled. "That's perfect."

As her hand grabbed the card, mine held tight. She tugged, but I didn't let go.

"Is there something wrong?"

I justified what I was doing on many different levels. Miss Regina Tor wasn't going to need her great insurance much longer. Hospitals already make so much money. And, finally, it wouldn't be the first time Gramma's age was lied about.

"Nothing." Everything. Then I let go of the card and committed medical fraud and identity theft. It was just that easy.

So why, when Lucy left the room, did I feel like I'd just betrayed not just my moral code, but Gramma's?

Chapter Nineteen

Radio

THEN

Sit-Rep: My plan to steal back my IDs is as lost as Riley's gold tooth. I am nine steps from the front door with no ride. Fierce, icy wind means I won't make it far on foot. Riley's keychain is dangling from his front right pocket. I can charge the sheriff now and get my ID, or I can sit down and sneak Riley's keys out. Both are untenable.

Since the sheriff has the upper hand, I grab the closest stool to him and try to squeeze a little power back for myself. I tilt my beer up and take a swig. "What's on your mind?"

"Why a girl like you needs a fake ID."

"What makes you think one is a fake?"

He chuckles. "Answering a question with a question only suggests you're hiding something,"

I finish my beer. "Kinda like the way you answered my question about what was on your mind."

He rubs his beard and tips his hat at me. "I'll be seeing you around, Ms. Craddock."

The sheriff sweeps over to a table with two empty beer cans and tosses them in the trash. That might be a considerate move, or it might be intentionally avoiding me as he puts his hand on the doorknob.

"Wait!" I shout, with no further plan of action than that one word.

The sheriff doesn't even turn around as he opens the door. A blast of cold air forces itself in. He uses his hat to block his face from the brunt of it just as the radio on his hip squawks.

He detaches it and steps outside.

Shit.

Sit-Rep: The sheriff is gone with my IDs. Depending on how slow or how fast the county's fax and phone service is, I'm possibly as screwed as Blanche Devereaux during Fleet Week. He might figure out that Patricia Ann Craddock *is actually* Ruth Olivia Kellum. *I mean, I did list the same home address on both of them. A little sleuthing and I'm done for.*

An icy beer slides down from the end of the bar and stops perfectly in front of me.

"How do you do that?" I ask as I pop the top.

"Look at the bottom."

I raise the beer can and study the rim of the bottom. As I run my finger along it, it sticks to my finger.

"Salt?"

"Sugar." Stalin strolls behind the bar and runs a wet dishrag around its wooden top. "Leaves a sticky residue, but so does a spilled beer." The big man chews on a toothpick as he extends his hand. I catch his drift and put a buck in it.

"That'll be two fifty."

"It's Schlitz." I take a swig. It takes a second before a harshness that is a cross between piss and antifreeze hits my throat. "You should be paying me to drink it."

Stalin laughs. "I like you, Ru-Ru. Or Rook. Or whatever you want me to call you."

"Rook is fine. Do I call you Stalin or Battleship?"

"Whichever floats your boat." The sound of heavy rain mixed with sleet pelts the bar's tin roof. Its intensity shifts every few minutes from nearly nonexistent to a downpour. "You know, not to be too forward, but if you need a place to stay, I've got a cot upstairs. That's all yours, but ole Cotton over there might insist on cuddling with you."

While I appreciate the guy's hospitality, I can't trust him. In my whole life, only one person ever truly had my back. And I lost her and that life about a year ago.

"I'll pass."

"Hey, just so you know, you don't have to worry about me." Stalin steps back but keeps his gaze on me. "I, well, play for the other team. And drive on the other side of the road."

While I know what he means, part of me just wants to watch how many anecdotes he will come up with.

"You know, I prefer hotdogs over burgers—"

"I get it," I interrupt, not ready for the next comparison. "You're three letters, one syllable. You can say gay, you know."

The defeated look on Stalin's face tells me he can't openly say it. Or at least not with company he doesn't know. That's why I am the one to break eye contact.

"You can come stay with me," Riley snickers. He takes a pull of his beer and winces less than before.

I guess his gums are getting numb.

"Oh, on that, it's a *hard* pass."

"What? I won't do anything to you."

And the only way to guarantee that is by not going with you.

Just then, the door to the bar opens. The sheriff reenters.

"It just came across the radio that we need to stay indoors for the next hour. Seems the storm's gonna shift to a squall soon enough."

Riley asks the obvious question. "What the hell is a squall?"

The sheriff slides his gun down to Stalin as the bartender slides a cold beer at the same time. The two pass each other without the slightest touch.

"Flurries have gusts of wind, that's where you have mere seconds of hard wind." He pops the top and takes a swig. "Now a squall, well, that's where you have minutes of hard, aggressive, attacking wind. A gust that can knock a car off the road. A squall can rip a roof off a house."

Just then, the metal roof moans, as if it supports the sheriff's prediction.

"Well, that's not good." Stalin opens a beer for himself, walks to the front door, and flips the wooden sign hanging in the window from *Stop Sta'lin and Get in Here!* to *Damn! We Closed.*

From next to the jukebox, Stalin grabs a deck of cards.

Without missing a beat, the sheriff and Riley take two of the empty chairs.

"I've got an hour of poker in me," says the sheriff through gritted teeth as he chews a toothpick.

I take the last chair.

Everyone else is here to play poker.

I'm here to get my license, get some keys, and get the hell out of here.

Chapter Twenty

The Shed

NOW

The ax handle slides back into the blade after a couple of shoves and a slap. I wind up resting the ax next to the cabin. I don't need it to cut anything yet. There are enough downed limbs and logs that I can carry and others I drag to a spot next to the cabin. Just near the southeast corner is an extension from the roof, kind of like a small awning. Beneath it is earth that is mostly clear of ice. I would carry the wood straight in, but I'll let Riley help me chop it into smaller pieces.

During one trek, I notice that the shed door is ajar. I guess Riley is still in there. Or maybe he already grabbed the tools he needed and went inside to fix the window.

It isn't until I hear a drill from inside the cabin that I realize he's definitely inside the cabin. As I glance around, something tickles my curiosity and I walk over to the shed. As expected, a thin layer of ice covers the door. I try to move it wider so I can slip inside, but the base holds to the ground like a grudge. From under my arm, I grab the flashlight and shine a beam in.

Inside the shed is what you would expect to find: an old lawnmower in the back with fishing poles stacked on top of it. Shelves with paint cans just above the mower. On the side walls is a hanging rack for tools. One side has repair tools like hammers, screwdrivers, and wrenches. The other has gardening tools such as shovels and hoes.

Across the floor is a blue tarp covering a good six feet long by five feet wide area. This will come in handy when, not if, a tree limb crashes through the cabin's roof. I turn my flashlight back to the walls of tools and spot the greatest invention known to man: duct tape. This silver stickiness will hold practically anything together, including a tarp that is getting sleeted on.

I grab the tarp with one hand and pull. It slips from my grasp. The gloves might keep me warmish, but they're soaked. I wrap my hand around the tarp tighter and give it a hard tug. Nothing. Finally, I set the flashlight down lens first, so the only light in the shed comes from the waning crescent of the moon.

Better than nothing, I guess.

With two hands at my disposal, I plant my feet, squat, and heave. I slip on some ice, probably stuck in the grooves of my right boot, and slam my right shoulder into the ground. My other foot kicks the flashlight. It topples over and blasts a beam back under the tarp.

"Shit," I mumble in embarrassment more than pain. The tarp is now partially on me, and mostly free of whatever was holding it down.

I roll around on the ground, mainly moving my legs to see what I hurt in the fall, when my foot connects with something solid. I pull up the tarp and glance down at my two feet.

Caught directly in the flashlight's beam is another foot.

Chapter Twenty-One

Arthur Fox

LAST YEAR

I couldn't tell if it was fear, guilt, or a combination of the two, but my whole body ached. Everything from my fingertips to my toes were freezing, even though I saw nursing staff wiping their brows from the sudden change in weather.

For the rest of the day, I didn't see Secretary: Lucy again. Part of me wanted to ask if she was still on duty. The other part told that part to shut the hell up.

I found myself wandering the halls. At some point, I walked past the hospital's chapel. Then I walked by it again. And again. And again. Until I went through those double swinging doors.

The room was about twice as big as Gramma's living room. Two stained glass windows above an altar greeted me. One had a Cross on it, the other the Star of David.

I bet the altar faces toward Mecca.

I knelt before the altar. My knees sunk down on the cushion, and I lowered my head.

What have I done?

That's when I felt a tap on my shoulder.

"Jesus Christ!" Startled, I turned and came face-to-face with the oldest white preacher I've ever seen.

"No, Arthur Fox." The five-foot-nothing man with Coke-bottle-thick glasses gave me a tight smile barely visible under his full beard. "Actually, J.C. is my boss."

I shook my head and threw on my fakest smile. "I was just looking around."

"Uh huh." This man, seven inches shorter than me, chewed his cheek as he looked me up and down. "Hard to do that with your eyes closed. How can I help you, my child?"

My eyes dart between the man and the door out.

As if he read my mind, Pastor Fox said, "You're free to go, you know?"

"Am I?" I answered the question more for myself than him.

"I've met many a person here." The small man just started talking and grabbed a seat in the pew on the side. "From Rosa Parks to Minoru Yamasaki, I've met a lot of Detroiters."

"Who's the second name?" I asked.

"The man that designed the World Trade Center. And, just like Rosa, you're from here, I bet."

I asked, "Do you know any movie stars?" He shook his head.

Then, I guess because he was a preacher, I told Pastor Fox that Gramma and I were watching a movie about a preacher, Buck and the Preacher, *before we wound up in the hospital.*

"Never seen it." He raised his left eyebrow and asked, "Any good?"

"Pretty good," I said. "There is a scene where the preacher uses his Bible as a shield."

"Well, while I abhor violence, I must say that the Good Book has saved me many a time as well."

"From bullets?"

"From myself."

An alarm on his Casio watch beeped and Pastor Fox silenced it. "I've got to make my rounds, but I can tell you are searching for something. I can't tell what it is, but I hope it finds you."

"Well, you know what the Bible says," I began. "God helps those that help themselves."

And I thought that was the end of the conversation, but Arthur Fox put his veiny-yet-firm hand on mine. He wasn't quite done with me yet.

"Actually, that's closer to a Quran scripture than Biblical, but you're only saying half of it."

He grabbed both of my shoulders and turned me to face him, dead center.

"I prefer the version which often credited to Algernon Sidney: God helps those who help themselves, but God help those who get caught helping themselves."

Well, God help me indeed.

Chapter Twenty-Two

Deal

THEN

We all sit around a square folding table next to the remains of the wooden one I broke with Bekkahh's back.

"So, why were you two ladies fighting?" asks Stalin as he glances at his broken table and shuffles the deck, a popping of crisp cards filling the air.

"The dumbest reason to."

"Does this reason have two heads and only thinks with one?" the sheriff asks.

"Ding-ding-ding we have a winner."

"Well, he clearly wasn't one," Riley says, managing to ooze creepiness from his attempted swagger. "Girl, I mean, you're one hell of a prize."

"I'm no one's prize except my own, Riley."

"Damn right, sweetheart." Stalin puts the deck in front of me. I cut it and lay the half-deck in front of the dealer.

"We're like two peas in a pod..." Riley flashes his eyes as he downs a gulp of beer. "Rook and Riley, like R&R whiskey. Rich and Rare."

More like Rogue and Redneck.

"Oh, I've had that shit," says the sheriff. "It should stand for rough and rowdy."

So have I. Just the thought of it makes my stomach ache.

"Ha!" Riley puts his hand on my shoulder.

At the look I send him, he promptly takes it back. I glance at the ceiling fan that wobbles with one blade in it. "Stalin, why's that fan so lonely?"

"You ever heard the expression *the shit hits the fan?*"

"I've lived it."

Stalin points his beer bottle up. "That particular piece of shit was Jason Thrasher. He was bullying a friend of mine, so I got his help in examining the durability of those blades." Stalin takes a swig. "The fan fared much better than the bully."

With that, Stalin deals.

"So, what are we playing?" I ask.

"It sure as hell ain't *Go Fish*, Ms. Craddock." There's a little quip in the sheriff's voice. He is having a blast with my fake name.

"Poker, Omaha-style."

"Shit, no, Battleship." Riley hops up from the table. "That hurts my head."

"I'm sure any level of cognitive reasoning does that," Stalin says with a chuckle.

"Naw, we need to play it simple: Five-card draw."

Stalin pats Riley on the hand. "And would you like a straw with your sippy cup?"

"Let's let the lady choose."

Maybe asking for my input is good manners, but I suspect he's really trying to gauge my level of poker skill. Some people think poker skills are genetic. I call bullshit. I made my own skills, because my uncle's poker addiction was what put Gramma in debt to begin with. I can't count the times I had to be dealt in a hand to try to win back some of the debt Uncle left on us.

Sometimes you fight fire with a bigger blaze.

"Let's keep it simple then," I say, "five card."

"And..." Riley darts to behind the bar. "And-and-and..."

"Get out of my bar, you asshole." Stalin's command is more of a grumpy complaint rather than an order. "You're not using up my Tabasco and top-shelf tequila for TNTs like last week."

"Well, if those are the rules, then hold up, dammit." Riley grabs four shot glasses from the shelf above the liquor. He sizes up the bottles as he points at each label.

"And don't go using my good shit if you're doing what I think you're doing." A panicked look crosses Stalin's face as his eyes go wide. "And no rum!"

"Why no rum?" I ask.

"Because the last time I shot rum, I wound up with a tattoo of Q*Bert blowing Pac-Man."

The silence that follows that comment is well justified. I clear my throat before I ask the next obvious question.

"From the Atari games?" I ask, trying and failing to hold in a chuckle. Stalin nods, his eyes not meeting mine.

"Dear God, man, why?" asks the Sheriff, voicing the question we're all thinking.

"Look, I lost a bet, okay?" Stalin crosses his arms and looks away. "For you prudes out there, I've had it altered. Now it just looks like Q*Bert is really, really, REALLY enjoying eating a pizza that is missing a slice."

"Can—can I see it?" I ask, trying to keep it together. *Don't-laugh-don't-laugh-don't-laugh.*

"You may not."

"Is, um, is it anywhere delicate?" asks the sheriff, as he rubs his cheeks, trying to pull them down from his eyes. Both the sheriff and I make eye contact but break away before our laughter dams break.

"That'd be a little, um, more intimate than either of us would feel comfortable with, Sheriff."

"Point taken."

After a few moments of glorious silence, the laughter starts with me. Then the sheriff, and finally Stalin. In this moment, all is right with the world.

"Ah freakin' ha!" Riley disappears under the bar and then comes up with a brown jug with the words *Entrepierna Del Diablo* on it. He holds it skyward.

"That's an idea." The sheriff shakes his head. "I wouldn't recommend we take it."

"Hell no." The words creep out of Stalin's throat flat yet accepting. It's like when your friend cuts her own hair and asks you how it looks. You try to sound supportive and accepting, but you're also trying not to scream *Dear God, why?*

"I mean, you use it to clean the tables, but it's still technically liquor."

I say, "That is the worst product slogan ever."

"So's Dr. Tichenor's mouthwash, but drinking either of those may lead to blindness."

"Also, we need..." Riley ignores the sheriff's last comment as he dashes over to the condiments. "Got it!" He grabs a small red bottle with a white label that reads *Delta Fire* on it. "And we're playing Arson Rules as well."

"Shit, son, you've got the sense of a dead dog," the Sheriff says.

I notice that's not a *no*.

"What are Arson Rules?" I ask as Riley puts the jug, four shot glasses, the Delta Fire hot sauce, and a glass of water on the table next to us.

"Simple," he answers. "The winner shoots water. The losers shoot tequila. Depending on how badly you lose, that's how spicy your shot will be. You come in second, that's one dash of *Delta Fire*. Next to last gets you three dashes. And last gets you five dashes."

Sit-Rep: If the sheriff gets drunk enough, I can sneak my licenses out of his pocket.

"I'm in," I say and lean back in a deep stretch. "I mean, I'd hate to chicken out in front of you strapping young men."

"You need to get your eyesight checked," Stalin says. Then he curses to himself, bangs his fists against the table, and says, "Fine. Shit. Fine. Just a couple of rounds."

"I'm out." The sheriff pushes back from the table.

Time to play dirty.

"That's fine, Sheriff," I say as the Sheriff stands. "I'm sure Riley's just betting that you're a shitty poker player that can't handle a drink stronger than beer."

I run my finger down the top of Riley's hand and give his pinky finger a little squeeze.

"Yeah, sheriff, there's no harm in saying when you're licked," adds Riley, taking the bait.

The cop glances me over. He knows I'm goading him.

Then he checks his watch and sits back down. "Deal, dammit."

Chapter Twenty-Three

What Cost?

LAST YEAR

For thirty minutes, I moved along the hospital's hallways having the worst conversation with myself. The angel on one shoulder and the devil on the other one kept strangling each other because there was no *right* answer.

Ultimately, I got myself into this jam, and I am damn sure I can get myself out.

I find Gramma awake in her chute. A glazed-over look of confusion and panic went across her face. She was tugging at the IV implanted in the top of her wrist. I caught her as the tape started ripping off her arm.

"Gramma, hey, it's okay!" I took her hands in mine. A small trickle of blood dripped from the spot where she'd yanked off the tape. I forgot how thin her skin was these days.

"Like Hades it is, I want out of here..." Then Gramma pushed my hands from hers and nodded to her purse on the sink. "Get my purse, I'll get my shoes."

"Gramma, you aren't well."

"Um-hmm..." Gramma chuckled, then coughed. She started fiddling with these nipple-looking attachments on her body that connected to some sort of heart monitor. "Just because I'm not ready to race don't mean I'm a lame horse."

Gramma smiled, sarcastic and tight-lipped. "Why don't you go ask the nurse to call me a cab?"

I took this as a challenge and went straight to the nurses' station. No one was around. As if a gift from God, I grabbed the stack of folders in the To Be Filed *bin. None of them carried my grandmother's name.*

Shit.

"Miss?" It was about that time that a nurse tapped me on the shoulder. I jumped so high I could see the dust on the lightbulbs. "I didn't mean to startle you, but your grandmother's room is now ready."

Instead of relief in my heart, I had ice running through it.

But at what cost?

Chapter Twenty-Four

Crazies

THEN

The first hand of poker goes like it should: I win. I should've; poker was the way I made money in high school. Sure, it's a game of chance, but, more than anything, it is a game about knowing your opponent.

As I shoot my shot of water, everyone else drinks spicy, shitty tequila. Poor Riley came in last with a six of clubs high. He's trying to blow out the fire in his mouth on his long-sleeve shirt that has *Rumors Bar and Grill* on it.

We're midway into the second hand before Stalin starts the small talk.

"Sheriff, anybody doing anything crazy in this weather?"

"So far, people are hunkering down and staying in, though I did hear about a fight at the Piggly Wiggly over Milk Bread."

"Some of those pairs of words don't go together," I say discarding a six and a four and fishing for another queen. "Look, I can do that, too. Siamese parrot. Pepto porkchop."

"Lots of milk and lots of bread. It's what people in the South buy in bulk at the sign of the first flurry." Stalin chuckles to himself and adds, "Hell, someone should just go town-to-town selling the duo when the clouds come in."

"Was it a good fight?" asks Riley, oddly hopeful. He's probably the kind of guy that loves watching a good fight but runs from them in real life.

"Well, I'd love to say *no*," answers the sheriff as he only tosses in one card. "In all honesty, it was a nail-scratching-hair-pulling-getting-beat-with-your-own-shoe kinda scrap. Okpunichi County's sheriff told me they thought they found part of a weave, but later realized it had some scalp still attached to it. Turns out that clump came from the manager trying to stop the fight."

"And that's why you don't break up a fight between two women!" Stalin tosses in four cards as Riley deals him four back. "I mean, they were women, right?"

"Can confirm. This weather, these two storm fronts hitting us at the same time, one hot, one cold, bring out the crazies in even the most docile of people."

As that line about *crazies* hangs in the air, I look around the table and wonder if I'm sitting with *crazies* as well.

Chapter Twenty-Five

Pictures

NOW

"Shit!" I don't even have time to cover my mouth as the word dashes from my throat. I crabwalk away as fast as possible, scurrying away from the shed.

The flashlight's beam is muffled under the tarp, so part of me wants to think I am making all this up. I have had a night straight out of *Reservoir Dogs* after all and am still probably a little drunk.

I push off the ground, stand, and dust myself off. *I am making this up.* I'm so convinced that my mind is playing tricks on me that I reach under the tarp, snag the flashlight, and point the beam around the shed instead of under the tarp.

Covering the floor are dozens of framed pictures of different sizes. As I shine the light around, I notice black-and-white wedding photos in one. Another is of a soldier in full uniform. One more is a kid and a father repairing what appears to be a watch. Then, of parents with a child all dressed in crazy outfits. A Halloween photo, because the father is dressed as a vampire, complete with dried blood, pale face, and a black cap. The mother is dressed in a white wedding gown with big black-and-white hair. I'm guessing *Bride of Dracula*, but she looks more like the *Bride of Frankenstein's monster* to me. And the little boy in a cowboy outfit, pistols drawn and aimed at the camera.

So that's where all the pictures went.

But why?

I stretch in the falling sleet, take a deep breath, and raise the tarp. As the flashlight's beam initially shows me that there is nothing to worry about, directly in front of me is something black. It's the bottom tread of a heavy-duty work boot. The tarp covers the rest of it, which means it might just be a boot. Still, I won't know the truth until I lift it.

Just as I do, the wooden handle of the ax slams down over the tarp.

Chapter Twenty-Six

The World Shifts

THEN

I wound up second this hand. The sheriff beat me with a full house versus my three-of-a-kind.

Riley, again, lands at last place.

I hadn't noticed until now that the tequila wasn't like other liquor I'd seen. It doesn't exactly pour out of the jug; it *glubs* out. There's a thickness to it that's not natural. It sort of reminds me of *The Blob* movie, well, the blob that ate everyone.

Then I do a dumb thing and smell the tequila.

"Oh, good Lord, it smells like antiseptic and rat shit."

Stalin studies the bottle. "Yep, that's on the ingredients label." Stalin tosses a dash of *Delta Fire* into my shot glass, three into his own, and five into Riley's. "Salute!"

"Salute!"

Upon drinking, there was a split second before the burning of cheap liquor or antifreeze punched my tongue. The burn of cayenne pepper, vinegar, and chili powder dances through my chest. I swear this trio pumps smoke into my lungs. I choke, which brings tears.

Then I swallow this lump and cough for thirty seconds, trying not to puke like I'm possessed in *The Exorcist*.

"W-w-why?" More coughs fight their way out of my body. "Why, uh, why would anyone drink that?"

Riley finishes his own coughing fit and adds, "Because the more flammable it is, the more potent it is."

I grab the last bit of my beer and down it to chase this demon down my throat, but all the beer does is make the throat-demon angry.

Stalin has kept his mouth shut for a few seconds after he finished his shot. His prize for the last hand was one part shitty tequila and three dashes of hellfire. As his body rumbles, he screams, "Aakakachu!"

I ask, "What the hell was that?"

He wipes his eyes with his sleeve and says, "I did that to try to cut the harshness of that shit."

"Did it work?" asks Riley, speaking on behalf of the entire bar.

He pauses before answering. "It did not..."

Riley shuffles the deck. "You know, on base, we made our own booze."

"Yeah, for toilet wine." I couldn't help myself. The tequila is making me less worried about life, the universe, and everything else. Plus, I may be having more fun.

"Naw, well, kinda. We used an old tub..."

"And that's why everyone at Camp Shelby went blind?" asks Stalin.

"Can I finish?"

"Would you stop talking if I said *no*?" asks the sheriff.

Riley sends him a wink and a smirk.

"So, anyway, we took bleach to clean out the tub, some hydrochloric acid to get rid of stains, and got some fruit, water, yeast, and let it sit."

"I'm pretty sure that's not how you make drinkable alcohol," I counter.

"Hey, if you drink it and don't die, it's drinkable."

"When you keep your bar low, you'll never fail, I guess." Stalin takes a beat and sits back in his chair. "You're not in the military, Riley. You didn't make it through Basic Training. That's like saying you played pro football yet never made a game."

"Hey, if you get cut from the major leagues, you still were in the major leagues," counters Riley." I learned a lot in those ten days so, yeah, I was military."

"I don't think that's how it works, Riley," says Stalin.

"I don't think you know what you are talking about and you can suck my balls, Battleship." Riley deals each of us our cards. "Unless you're into that."

"No one wants to suck balls, Riley, no matter their sexual orientation." Stalin adjusts his cards and puts them in some order only he understands.

"Amen," I add. I fling two cards at Riley.

He replies with a creepy, tight smile.

"Also, Riley, you keep losing teeth to stupid shit like opening beer bottles, the last thing you'll need to worry about is anyone finding you attractive."

"That's mean, girl." Riley deals me two cards so fast they scoot across the table and wind up in my chest. "I'm gonna remember that."

"I didn't say it so you'd forget."

At first, I think a rumble from distant thunder was in the air. Then I hear a dog bark, and I glance over at the lab in the corner. It seems the pup farted so loud it woke her up. Then she yelled at her ass and rolled over.

"Down, Cotton, down!" Stalin chuckles before adding, "We've got company, lil lady."

This hand, I come in third, earning an extra-spicy shot. I down it, then pretend to drink my beer while actually spitting the shot out in the can.

"That's alcohol abuse, Ms. Henry." The sheriff takes my can, turns it upright, and pours it back into my shot glass. "Salute."

I shoot it. And that's when the world shifts on its axis and I forget the real reason I'm playing poker.

Chapter Twenty-Seven

The Main Person I'd Wronged

Last Year

Wouldn't you know it? That day, Gramma got moved up in the schedule. Next thing we knew, she met with the specialist and two other doctors at 3:00 P.M. They did a CT scan, EKG, and I think other three-letter tests as well. They even put in a temporary stint, which wasn't nearly as complicated a procedure as TV shows made it out to be.

Unfortunately, she was still hooked to enough machines to make Darth Vader appear naked, but it was a great improvement from our previous conditions.

The cardiologist said that Gramma had indeed had a heart attack: a non-ST segment elevation myocardial infarction. All of those made-up-sounding words meant Gramma hadn't gotten enough oxygen and her heart tried to jump ship. It was not as serious as an ST segment elevation myocardial infarction, one where the arteries and blood flow were damaged or not doing their damn job. Still, the cardiologist patted Gramma on the back.

"Don't worry; we'll be monitoring you closely."

And that's what good insurance did: gained Gramma human decency.

She met with a dietician, a person who apparently told you what you should eat. That didn't sit well with Gramma. When he asked her if she cooked with olive oil, canola oil, or anything other than dairy, it didn't go great.

"I was raised on the butter, son, and you'll take it away from my cold, dead hands."

I told the guy I'd work on Gramma, which he knew meant a big fat "no" would still be the answer.

The next morning, I was working with Gramma on a breathing game when the weather kicked up. We'd heard about the possibility of a storm but, with everything Gramma was going through, I hadn't given it a second thought.

Strong winds slapped against Gramma's private room's window. Next to us, a crane, the kind used to move beams, rocked back and forth. I leaned back to Gramma as she was trying to suck a ball through a tube. This physical therapy device's treatment featured three balls in a plastic container. Each was in its own cylinder and, under each ball, was a tube. With a little inhalation, Gramma would make one ball float. With a deeper inhale, she could do the same to the second. And with the deepest of breaths, she might make the last ball float.

Currently, we were stuck at the first ball.

"Lil Hoody, take this torture device away from me." Gramma pushed it away. "I don't need it."

"*Gramma, you do.*" I angled the nozzle toward her face. She then jerked her head away. "*If you get the second one, you get an extra pudding.*"

She crossed her arms like a toddler who refused to eat her green beans. "*If I weren't your gramma, I'd tell you where you could shove that pudding.*"

"*Then do it.*"

"*Nope.*" She shook her wigless head. "*Wouldn't be Christian.*"

"*But would it be fun?*" I grinned.

After a second, she looked around as if she were looking for Jesus Christ himself. Not finding Our Lord and Savior, she whispered her answer.

"*Your butt.*" As she said this, her heartbeat monitor showed a rise in her rhythm.

I guess it was all the stress or turmoil or pure, unadulterated bullshit that we'd dealt with the last few days. Hearing my 64-year-old grandmother say 'your butt' sent me to the floor. I hadn't laughed that hard since my high school bully Laurnell Johnson got her weave caught in the school bus' door.

But this time was different. I kept laughing. For the life of me, I couldn't stop. Then the tears flowed. The laughs became sobs, which became gasps. I shook as my body was a kettle screaming past the boiling point. The next logical step was to overflow.

Gramma's hand brushed my neck. She said, "Oh, Lil Hoody, you're going to be fine."

That's so unfair. Gramma was fighting for her life, yet she was thinking about others. Me.

"Oh, Gramma, please don't get out of bed." I wiped away the tears and jumped to my feet. "You have to take easy."

"And so do you." She put both of her hands on my face and gave me a squeeze as her eyes met mine. "I'm not the only one in this hospital bed."

In this moment, everything was okay. Gramma was on the road to recovery. I didn't feel so alone.

The wind outside kicked up, and the lights flickered. Once. Twice.

Gramma's heartbeat ramped up, clocking close to a hundred. Her new heart stints must be working well.

"Hey, Gramma, like you said, everything is okay..."

She smiled, then her numbers went down.

And that's when I decided to come clean with the main person I'd wronged.

Chapter Twenty-Eight

Cracking

NOW

"Holy shit!" I stumble back as Riley taps the handle up and down on the tarp.

"Curious little kitty, ain'tcha?" Riley pushes the shed door closed and snaps shut the padlock. I don't know when he got the ax from the side of the cabin, but losing it to him throttles my pulse.

Also, how long was Riley watching me?

"I know what you were doing."

I try to hide my surprise. Even I'm not completely sure what I was doing, but if what is in the shed is what I think it is, I'm dead.

"You're trying to find lighter fluid."

The sense of relief that covers my body makes me forget I'm currently freezing. "Guilty, Riley."

He slaps his leg and says, "You know a good ole country boy can light a fire without it, girl! I was born to burn! Come on."

As we walk back toward the cabin, I can't help but look at the shed and wonder what other secrets are in that tiny house.

And that's when the sound of trees shattering fills the air.

Chapter Twenty-Nine

World Isn't Crumbling Around Us

THEN

The power flickers, but only for a second.

"Stalin, you've got your generators running, don'tcha?" asks the sheriff.

"Never uninstalled them during the rezoning."

I'm too drunk to pussyfoot around this vague shit. "What the hell are you two talking about?"

"You don't know about rezoning where you're from?" asks the sheriff.

"Aren't they a band from Oxford?"

"No, dumbass. Every couple of decades, the State of Mississippi rezones some of its counties." Stalin takes a pull off his beer and continues. "It's mainly to shift votes and fix elections. But *this bar* and everything within a twenty-mile radius had just been left off because we are only a handful of voters, and some of us are felons who can't vote."

"Then how do you get things like electricity?" I ask.

"I pay gas and electricity to Mississippi Power & Light, but some of our few residences pay Rural Light & Power. And I forgot to mention The Compound."

"What's the Compound?"

"The Compound, well, that's a story for another day..."

I realize how dry my throat is and take a deep swig on an empty beer, coming up with nothing but a dryer mouth. "Hold that thought as I grab another. Anybody want one?"

All hands shoot up. Drunk as a skunk, I close one eye and use my pointer finger and count hands.

"Got it. Please continue." I dart to the cooler and this time the sheriff jumps in.

"This area got zoned before satellite imagery. That meant a human went and zoned everything. Turns out, it was last zoned in 1943 by a man that was half blind and mostly illiterate."

I pop open three Miller Lites since we drank all the Coors. *I just hope Stalin doesn't get mad.* I return to the table and hand out all the bottles.

Stalin says, "So, this county came into unofficial existence twenty-nine years ago. Yet, we pay no taxes to any courthouse. No school taxes. Nothing. It is heavenly."

"Isn't the State of Mississippi gonna miss their money?" I ask.

"The next smallest county in The 'Sip is four hundred square miles, and we're less than one tenth that size. Even though we're tiny, I'm sure the tax collectors will come for us at one point." Stalin tears his beer label and flicks it on the floor. "The gub-ment will always come for what they want."

"If that's the case about not paying taxes, why hasn't everybody moved here?" I ask.

"It's too remote." The sheriff leans forward and taps his beer's bottom on the table. "There's miles between homes. Creates a sense of loneliness, or strandedness, that comes with living away from people."

The Miller I gulp down is much sweeter and thinner than the Coors. That just means I can drink more of it, I guess.

"That must suck in an emergency. Like, if you needed to get some-one to a hospital or something, it'll take longer."

While I knew I was leaning up against *my* fear of hospitals, I never expected the sheriff to be the one to tear up.

"Oh shit! Did I say something?"

The sheriff just shakes his head.

Stalin pats him on the back and says, "Two years ago, someone murdered Sheriff's wife and daughter when he was out."

"Oh my God!" I lean across the table and grab this stranger's hand. "I am so sorry!"

The cop slips his hand out and grabs his beer. After a pull, he says, "I tell myself that I couldn't've stopped it even if we lived in town where it is safer." He takes a larger gulp and adds, "I'm good at lying to myself."

Then he points at Stalin.

"I'm not lying." Stalin angles his beer bottle to a picture above the bar. It is a black-and-white photo of a young lady with a small boy. I instinctively go up to it. If the power did go out in the bar, her smile would light the room. Oddly, while the picture looks like it is in great shape, there is a smudge in the white part of the lady's eye.

As I wipe the dust from the glass, I ask, "Who's this?"

"My mother." Stalin clears his throat and the chair shifts under his weight. "She went missing when I was a boy. The insurance company said they wouldn't pay. No body, no check, if you get my drift. It's a million-dollar policy, plus any interest it's made since some of it is linked to the stock market." Stalin lets out a sigh. "Every year, I write those bastards a check for thirty-nine damn dollars to keep the policy active."

"I hate the way the pictures look at you," Riley chimes in, "into your soul, like they're judging you because you're not stuck in time and they are."

"Cooter, remind me to never look at a scrapbook with you," says Stalin.

"What if your mother is still alive?" I ask, my filters completely in the *off position*. "I mean, what if she just ran away? What would you do if she just came home?"

"Then I will be the happiest son in the world."

"Mothers are complicated creatures," Riley, of all people, says, "that we are taught to love because we fear the unknown."

"Damn, Cooter." Stalin rubs his chin and adds, "I'd expect that from the sheriff."

"Why?" asks the sheriff. "I thought everything I did screamed I am all about Laidback Lawman."

"Now, that's a band name!"

As we laugh, a loud crash occurs outside. None of us jump. Instead, the sheriff grabs the cards and shuffles. We go about our business, as if the world isn't crumbling around us.

Chapter Thirty

Miss Regina

Last Year

I stood outside of Miss Regina Tor's door for what felt like an eternity. The door had a push-down doorknob, the kind that you could easily hit with your butt if you were carrying something. As I cracked it open, a dead-flower-and-sea-salt smell hit me. The overhead lights were off, save for the mandatory one on the patient's face. I timed my steps to coincide with the beats of the machines that were monitoring Miss Regina.

Miss Regina, though just slightly older than my Gramma, looked like a corpse in a movie. With her sunken features and glazed-over eyes, maybe she looked more zombie than human. Her hair was mostly gone, with only a few strands here and there dangling off the sides of her skull. Her mouth was open, but the trickles of air going in and out of her lungs were so minor that, at times, it looked like she wasn't breathing at all.

In the corner of her room, with an uneaten tray of food on a rolling table between me and it, was Miss Regina's purse. I grabbed the rolling cart, but it wouldn't move. The wheels were locked. Using my foot, I angled out and released three of the four wheels with three small presses. The last one was not giving, despite the number of times I clicked it.

Just like the wheels on a shopping cart: one's gonna make everything wonky.

I took the next minute to tug the damned thing a few inches until the locked wheel would squeak. Then I'd stop, wait, and repeat. At the end, I had a clear path to the purse.

Booyah.

I opened the polka dotted purse about the size of a hardback book. There, I saw foundation, lip gloss, lipstick, powder, and a pack of tissues. I dropped Miss Regina's wallet in. It fell with an unsatisfying whump.

Once I put the wallet and purse back in the chair, I felt a little tug on my shirt.

It was a hand.

"H-h-hello?"

I fell back into the wall. "Shit!" I'd planned on apologizing to her, but now that I found her awake, I wasn't so sure. Sightless eyes somehow focused on me. A heart monitor beeped louder than before. I waited for it to sound an alarm and for them to catch me.

"Miss Regina, wow, I'm sorry. I didn't mean to disturb you." A lie, but a well-meaning one. *"I did a bad thing."*

Miss Regina looked more through me than at me when she said, "S-s-stay with me."

"Ma'am." In my gut, I knew the closed door would open and I would be caught. "Ma'am, I don't think you heard me. I...stole from you..."

Then Miss Regina's eyes looked down at my hand. "S-s-stay with me."

And I did. If Miss Regina couldn't comprehend my words, she might understand my actions. I took that empty seat. And I held Miss Regina's hand until her eyes closed and her breathing returned to almost non-existent levels.

I wish I could say I did this because I was kind. I'm not. I stole from this lady.

After she fell asleep, I quietly shut Miss Regina's door and snuck toward Gramma's room.

And that's when I found the door shut.

Chapter Thirty-One

Keep Someone Out, or Keep Something In

NOW

A sound like a million bags of popcorn popping fills the air. In every direction, the limbs and trees buckle, swaying as if an invisible gust of wind hits them head-on. Then they break.

The first casualty crashes directly on the tool shed. The aluminum structure drops in height by half as an entire tree flattens it. A minute earlier, and it would have killed me.

Then it takes an idiot to state what I should obviously be doing.

"Run!" Riley screams this as he grabs my hand and drags me toward the cabin.

A limb falls right between us, breaking our grasp, but luckily not our arms.

I jump over it as two more fall. Another clips my shoulder, changing my path. I kick off of a downed limb as thick as a garbage can and keep going. Riley holds open the door as I dodge more falling trees, their limbs whipping my arms and slicing small cuts in my face.

"Hurry! Run!"

"I'M RUNNING DAMN YOU!"

Just as I make the steps, a limb crashes down, blocking my path. I crawl over it and barely make it through as a tree crushes that limb.

We dart inside and get under an interior doorframe, the one next to the kitchen. Limb after limb crashes on the roof, their pounding worse than our car crash. Even with hand-covered ears, the auditory assault overwhelms me. The lights in the house flicker with each strike, until everything goes dark. Both of us huddle together and brace for this old cabin's roof to cave in. The sound reminds of me watching *Twenty Thousand Leagues Under the Sea* with Gramma. It's when the Nautilus goes deeper and deeper, and the pressure on the hull collapsing and the fear of everything crashing in had me chewing on my fingernails.

Then, the falls slow. A few more thuds occur, but nothing like before.

As Riley and I huddle nose to nose, I break the tension the only way I know how.

"I think we just got more firewood."

Riley laughs, then he kisses me. There's a scruffiness to his stubble that stabs my skin. His entire body smells of beer and sweat. All this, from the way he smells to the way we cling to each other, reminds me of the backseat where I lost my virginity. I was fifteen, and he was seventeen. I was a nerd. He was a jock. It was the most stereotypical first time ever. Afterward, we never spoke again.

For the life of me, I can't even remember his name...

I'm too shocked to push Riley away, but I also do not embrace it. He pulls back first, and I send a quick, tight-lipped smile his way. It's not a welcoming one, more of a *well, that happened* one.

"I'm sorry." Riley scoots back, stands up, extends his hand to me, then takes it away to scratch his scalp. "I just got carried away."

"It's fine." *It's not fine.* As far as I'm concerned, *fine* just left the cabin screaming. The sooner I find my way out of this situation, the better.

"Well, with the power out, it's only a matter of time before the temp plummets." Riley opens the door and glances out. "I'll start breaking some of these up so we can warm up the place, if you'll light the stove and get the cocoa going?"

"On it."

The moment Riley closes the door behind him, I dart through the door into the attached and enclosed garage. I open the rusted door to the VW bug and look for keys. Not finding them in the ignition, I check the glove compartment. Nothing there.

Surely, they're not in the driver side visor, I think as I flick down the visor with one hand. Only it's a dead cockroach that lands in my hand instead of the keys. I fling it away.

Even if I had the keys, I might wait to escape. Riley's outside gathering wood. I can't guarantee he's not out front.

I leave the VW and head to the garage door. It's a pulley chain one that will work without power.

Thank you, Jesus.

As I pull on the chain, the door moans. Just like at Stalin's bar, the outside door is frozen shut. Luckily, I find a bottle of storebought de-icer on a shelf. Now all I have to do is sneak out the front and douse the door, and then maybe I can get out of here.

Leaving the garage, I spot a room at the end of the hall. I hadn't explored all the way down because I had to piss so badly.

As I walk down the plush greenish shaggy carpet, I see a door next to the bathroom. I open it to reveal a pretty dated little boy's room. Posters from Clint Eastwood-ish westerns from the early '60s. You know, the ones with titles like *Coogan, High Noon,* and even a *Blazing Saddles.* If a current kid lived here, I'd expect Clint's recent western, *Unforgiven,* on the wall, though that's not a movie for kids, I guess.

Embossed on the dresser across from a small bed is the lone word *Carolton.*

Ah, Riley. I guess if I was a boy named Carolton, I'd go by Carl.

I run my fingers along it and collect the dust, then blow it onto the mirror in the center. There's also a trophy for Most Improved Player with the name Carolton R. on it. The football player on it is striking the Heisman Pose, one leg up and one hand out, with the ball tucked close to his chest.

I shut the door and continue my trek. The floorboards under the carpet creak and some of the carpet bunches up under my shoe. As I get closer to the door at the end of the hallway, I cannot make out what is on it. Curse me for not grabbing my flashlight. As I feel around, I touch not one, but two metal padlocks in both the top and bottom segments of the door. The hinges are shiny gold without a scratch on them.

Is this room locked like this to keep someone out, or keep something in?

Chapter Thirty-Two

Dark Secret

NOW

I sprint to the kitchen and grab my flashlight. Along the way, I spot Riley outside through a frosted window, repeatedly hacking away with the ax on a downed tree in the backyard.

I return to look at the locks; they don't look very fancy. In fact, they look quite cheap, unlike the Master Lock on the tool shed. These plain silver-and-gold locks remind me of the kind teachers put on their desks in high school. Nothing says *break into me* like a lock on something. Those drawers were where we could always find candy, contraband, and even the almighty gradebook.

And I know how to handle those locks.

Sit-Rep: I should get the hell out of here. Whatever is in that room has nothing to do with me. However, something in my gut tells me I must get in there. If I am to get in there, I need to get through two padlocks. Luckily, all I need is a strong magnet because these are spring-loaded locks, like my teacher's.

Back in the kitchen, I check the fridge for a magnet. Apparently, this is the only home in America without knick-knacky magnets on a refrigerator. Of course, if I found one, it might not be strong enough to reset the springs.

Think, Rook, think.

My eyes dance along the kitchen counter until I see my miracle: a beige electronic can opener. I yank the power cable and first look at the plug. It's two pronged, not three.

This sucker is old.

And old things are powerful.

I examine the magnet under the top of the device. It's the size of a half dollar. I flip the flashlight over and put the base near it. Before I can brace, the magnet yanks the flashlight from my hand. It takes three good pulls before I get the flashlight free.

Perfect.

Then a red flag pops up in my head: as I cross the living room, I cannot see Riley through any window. *Shit.* He's probably moved on to another section of the yard. If I'm lucky, he'll clear the downed limbs and trees in the front yard blocking the road.

I laugh to myself. *I've never once been lucky, so why start now?*

I place the can opener's magnet next to the top lock. It *clacks* so loudly I feel it in my bones. I pull on the lock.

Nothing happens.

Shit. Maybe I should try the other side.

I plant my foot against the door to release the lock/can opener lover's embrace and push off, crashing to the ground.

This is my reminder that my middle name is Olivia, not Graceful.

Since I'm already on the ground, I line up the magnet on the bottom lock. Another *clack*. This time, the hinge of the lock swings open.

One to go.

Back on my feet, I yank the stuck lock from the can opener and toss it to the plush carpet. I place the magnet on the other side of the top lock. One final *clack*, and the magnet unlocks.

Bingo.

Then every bit of joy from this victory drains out of my body when I open the door and discover Riley's dark secret.

Part Two: Squall

The National Weather Service defines a squall as an intense, but limited duration, period of moderate to heavy snowfall, accompanied by strong, gusty surface winds and possibly lightning (generally moderate to heavy snow showers). Snow accumulation may be significant.

Caution Level: High

Chapter Thirty-Three

Help

NOW

The bedroom is bigger than the child's room. Probably double the size at least. The dark room only has a sliver of light coming into it through mostly drawn curtains. Part of me wants to open them to get a better view of what is in my flashlight's limited beam. However, Riley might spot the beam from outside, so I cut off the flashlight. There's just enough moonlight coming through that I should be able to see.

"Hello?" I ask, with no response.

In the dim light, I stumble toward the wall. Near the window, I touch a wooden piece of furniture with a bunch of glass bottles on it. I grab one and open it. A whiff of rose oil and cardamom floods my nostrils. *Perfume.* I open another and find a kind of cakey powder. *Foundation.*

I crouch and move along the wall. Suddenly, the wall ends. I step left and find a sink, then a small, separate bathroom. Next, I move toward the center of the room. On the far wall, my right knee connects with something hard and I curse as a slight pain moves up my thigh.

My fingers move along the comforter, moving along the old, rough wool, from the wooden footboard. *A bed.* Then my hand hits something solid. Metal. And cold.

Using both hands, I feel the object. Its roundish shape is more egg-like, and it makes a sloshing noise.

Then the smell hits me, and I almost throw up. It's a bedpan. I should've smelled it before, but I guess my senses are in overdrive in the dark. I move to the side of the bed.

My feet catch on something on the rug. As I move my foot around, the small object topples over. A shoe. As I lean down to pick it, I notice the shoe is small. It's a sneaker, about as long as my hand. Maybe a child's.

I drop it and extend my hand. It connects with a small, square pillow. There are tassels hanging from it, so it is a decorative pillow that people put on their beds and never actually sleep on.

Maybe I can use it to dim my flashlight and give me just enough of a glow to look around.

From my pocket, I grab the flashlight. I shove the front into the pillow, cut it on, giving me a torch-like effect.

Then try not to scream.

The corpse of an elderly lady, probably eighty or so, lies face up. Her eyes are open. I'm not sure what color they were in life, but right now they appear black as night.

I can't tell how long she's been here. I move my pillow-flashlight combo around the room. In the corner, I spot a TV tray full of dirty dishes and partially drunk water glasses.

Oh my God, what has Riley done?

Next to the bed, on the small wooden nightstand, I spot my salvation: a keychain. Those have to be the keys to the VW bug.

I reach for the keys.

Just as they jingle in my hand, an ice-cold grip locks around my wrist.

"Help."

Chapter Thirty-Four

Crane

Last Year

I walked to the shut door in a haze. Something in the bottom of my stomach knew that this door being shut was a bad thing. I knocked because I thought maybe a nurse was bathing Gramma or something.

That's when a voice way too masculine and deep for Gramma's replied, "Enter."

I opened the door to two tall men in suits and a man in an orange jumpsuit. The suits were both a good foot taller than me. The prisoner looked like their pet, hunched over and studying me with beady eyes.

"Lil Hoody, these men think either you or me have lied to the government for some strange reason." Layered in Gramma's snarky comment was a tremor. "I told them I don't remember filling out any forms."

Everything turned static in my brain. A white noise filled my ears. The men showed their badges, as if their black suits, white shirts, and thin black ties didn't already scream federal agents. I read their lips because the sound of my heartbeat was bass beating my brain and ears like they owed my heart money.

The agent on the left, the white guy with the tight crew cut, opened a manilla folder. Even though it was closed and blank on the outside, I knew exactly what was in it: my forged copy of fake insurance for Gramma.

The other agent, the bro with the high and tight 'fro worthy a Kid 'n Play music video, brought out the insurance form for Miss Regina.

I kept staring at the prisoner. His sunken eyes and wild white hair made him look more feral than human. His hands were cuffed. Attached to them was a chain to a matching set of cuffs on his ankles.

The Kid 'n Play fed snapped his fingers in front of my face, forcing my focus. "We've been told that Ms. Kellum here didn't fill out these forms or provide proof of insurance. We're told you did. Do you have any idea of the amount of trouble you are in?"

Part of me wanted to answer yes. I stared at the two authority figures before me in disbelief. It wasn't that they caught me; I'd expected that to happen. Just not so quickly.

I ask the guiltiest of all questions, "How'd you find out?"

"It wasn't us," replied Crew Cut. "We're just here on a prisoner transport and someone called in a favor, so we're doing double duty."

The static in my head returned. They said a few more things. Then I noticed they had stopped looking at me. Instead, they were looking over my shoulder. Out the window.

That's when I realized it wasn't static in my head. It was the sound of the storm hitting the building. Limb after limb slammed against the window until it cracked. It sounded as if a jet engine was ramping up for takeoff right next to Gramma's room.

The lights flickered. Even though it wasn't yet five P.M., the sky had turned black. A loud boom, like a bomb went off, came from outside, and the lights went out.

"Shit," said Crew Cut. "Transformer's blown."

"*Maybe.*" *Mister House Party's eyes darted between me and my Gramma. "This storm is making everyone crazy."*

The lights quickly came back on, but my attention was on the prisoner. He was bouncing side to side on the balls of his feet. I thought about saying something to the feds, but I was too shaken to do anything.

When the lights went out again, the prisoner took his shot. He shoved Kid 'n Play into me. We toppled backwards onto the floor, blocking the path for the white fed.

I'd never seen someone with so little freedom of movement move so fast.

"Dammit, we've got a runner..."

Kid 'n Play pushed off of me and headed to the door.

Crew Cut grabbed Kid 'n Play's arm and pointed at me. "What do we do with her?" he asked.

"Damn, man, I don't know."

Then, without another word, Crew Cut shook his head, grabbed a set of handcuffs from behind his back, and cuffed both of my hands to the end of my grandmother's bed.

"You can't handcuff a perp to the bed!" Kid 'n Play said.

"Do you have a better idea?" asked Crew Cut as he shot out the door. "We won't be gone a minute."

"Wait, you can't just leave me handcuffed here." I used my good hand to point at the window. "What about the storm?"

"I'm sure it will blow over." Neither agent turned to even nod goodbye as they entered the hallway and Kid 'n Play said, "Someone will come deal with you."

The moment they shut the door, something crashed down through the roof right where they were standing. As rain and sleet flooded in, I saw that the builder's crane had crushed those agents.

And sealed Gramma and me off from the rest of the hospital.

Chapter Thirty-Five

Out of Here

THEN

"You know what my favorite movie is?" asks Riley, as if anyone is dying to know what ranks number one in Rileyville. "*The Abyss.*"

"Good flick," concedes Stalin. "I like the idea that we can condition our lungs to breathe underwater."

"Never seen it," says the Sheriff with an emphasis that might mean *never going to.*

"My favorite part is the sea creature that can take any form." Riley smacks his lips and kicks back in the chair. "Yeah, I'd hit that poon tang."

I guess Riley didn't expect us to stare at him like he's a UFO, but that's what he gets.

"What?" Riley pushes back from the table. "Don't judge me! I'm all about new experiences and taking risks and living my life to the fullest might just mean smashing some Martian ass."

"Ain't you just a walking, talking Mentos commercial?" the Sheriff says.

I want to bust out laughing, but then something in my stomach turns sour. It might be the beer, or the hot sauce, or the table-cleaning tequila—or, more likely, a combination of all three of the little bastards.

The sheriff touches my shoulder. "You're looking pretty pink for a black girl."

"I'm fine," I lie. *I'm so not fine.* Somehow, I'm swaying in my chair.

Riley reaches into his pocket and pulls out a joint. It's one snaggly looking thing, like it's full of pocket lint and ball sweat. He winks at the sheriff and lights it up.

I still don't get why the sheriff is letting Riley get away with stuff. *What is their history?*

After a big puff, Riley blows the cloud straight into the sheriff's face. He swats it away with one hand, more of an awareness of the slight than being bothered by the cloud. "I love weed. LOVE it. My thing with it is I smoke some, then think, *man, I should take out my contacts.*"

I ask, "Do you wear any?"

"Nope! So, the next thing I know I'm clawing at my eyes completely naked listening to '40s swing music on my Walkman while the manager is trying to get me out of the McDonald's ball pit." He takes another puff. "So, that's Riley on weed."

"First of all, no one needs to see that tonight because the mental image alone is traumatic." Stalin yanks the joint from Riley, drops it to the hardwood, and stomps the sucker flat. "Secondly, if you're going to start speaking in third person, you can first-person your ass out the door."

"That was my last joint!" Riley crosses his arms. "Jesus Christ..."

"Was killed and resurrected," concludes Stalin.

By the next hand, I no longer taste anything. I have jelly legs and rubbery elbows. Riley is three full sheets to the wind. Stalin is giggly, which means his large lower body rumbles and his head bounces side to side like a little bobbing dog on a car's dash.

And the sheriff is as sober as a church mouse.

"Why aren't you getting sober, er, drunk, drunker, drunkererer?" I stumble through the sentence, hitting every obstacle along the way.

"I've got a tolerance."

"How so?"

"Mama started me young." The sheriff pulls out a pipe and a Zippo. The silver lighter makes a _snikt_ as he opens it on a downward strike against his jeans. Then he lights it on the upward strike. He closes it and places the lighter on the table. After two, then three puffs of tobacco, the room smells worlds better than hot sauce and tequila.

"My mother taught me a lot, including respect for the law. Not man's law, really. A Higher Power's law. Respect is too weak a word, really. I _cherish_ the law. And _cherish,_ well, _cherish_ comes from the Latin word _carus._ It does mean _beloved_ and _dear,_ like we might expect it to. But it also means _costly._"

"Had a feeling you were gonna tell a story," I say, slumping back and smiling, pretending that I didn't just hit my head on the back of the chair on the way. "Know why?"

"Why, Ms. Craddock?"

"Because you pulled out a pipe. No one in the history of the world has ever lit a pipe and then not told a story."

"Fact! Fact right there!" Riley's enthusiasm adds nothing to my point as he knocks the table hard with his knee. The cards spill into the sheriff's lap.

As the sheriff leans down to gather cards from the floor, I lean in *to help*. As I do, I grab some from under my seat. Then, as I lean up, my hand goes to the sheriff's front shirt pocket.

"Hold up, now." The sheriff takes my hand in his. He tries to pry open my hand.

"What the hell are you doing?"

"Open your hand, Ms. Craddock."

No one else at the table speaks. The mixture of ice and rain hitting the tin roof gets louder. Limbs of trees scrap the windows.

I try not to meet the sheriff's gaze.

"Open it."

"Fine." As I say the word, it stretches into four syllables, like I'm a kid at the dinner table who agrees to eat his peas. I open my hand. In it is the Ace of Spades. "Look, I'm not saying I was gonna use it. I just wanted the option."

"Uh-huh." The sheriff taps his shirt, feels for the license through the pocket, touches the plastic laminate, and buttons back up.

However, what he's feeling is that Two of Clubs I switched out for my licenses.

Now to get out of here.

Chapter Thirty-Six

Stopped Working

Last Year

The rain and sleet poured into our room through the opening made by the fallen construction crane. Underneath the crane and the rubble were two federal agents who had handcuffed me to the end of Gramma's bed.

It was like a dream. Lights, even the orange auxiliary power ones, flickered. Various alarms blared. Weather alert warnings on radios from the hallway squawked to seek shelter. Medical equipment that was losing power chirped, pleading, until ultimately fading away. Scared patients must've been hitting their useless Call Nurse *button because voices of all ages were yelling. It was chaos.*

"Help!" I kicked at the end of the bed, my prison, trying to get the handcuffs to release. They held firm. "Someone please help us!"

"Someone come get us!" Gramma's yell was equal parts request and command, a tone I knew well. Years of being raised by her had conditioned me to know that tone meant one thing: business.

However, business was not happening until someone moved the crane that separated us from the rest of the hospital.

No one was coming.

Then, for a moment, Gramma's room lit up. We had power.

"Gramma, hit the Call Nurse *button on your remote!"*

Gramma leaned over the right side of her bed, but the guard rail was in her way. She yanked out her IV drip to try to get closer. Her frail fingers stretched as far as her muscles and bones would allow, her perfectly manicured pink fingernails nicking the remote again and again. She couldn't reach our swaying savior.

And neither could I.

Then Gramma grunted and reached with all her strength. Her breathing was short, as if she was breathing through a straw.

"Gramma, on second thought, they'll come get us soon."

"Almost got it, Lil Hoody..."

Even from five feet away, the sweat that poured out of Gramma soaking her green hospital gown was visible. "Come here, you lil scoundrel..."

"Gramma, you've got to slow down."

"I-got-you-I-got-you..."

Then she did exactly that. She had the remote in her hand. The wide-eyed face on Gramma's kicked-back head screamed victory.

Right when she hit the call nurse button, the white lights switched to orange. Then those flickered and faded to black. In unison, all her machines ceased their panicked chorus. Every sound in the hospital faded away as those lifesaving machines stopped working.

And then so did Gramma's heart.

Chapter Thirty-Seven

I Cannot Scream

NOW

I fall to the floor with a thud. So does the frail lady. Her grip on my hand pulls all ninety pounds of her off the bed and she smashes into me and the bedpan crashes to the ground. The smell of old piss and shit overwhelms me, though it is not coming from the spilled bedpan. Riley clearly hasn't bathed his hostage, and until now, the comforter had stifled the stench.

Her breath reeks of bile and something fruity. The dropped flashlight blasts its beam straight at us. Even though the light should blind her, the lady's eyes are wide. And dilated. Her eyes are a mixture of bloodshot and jaundiced. Then she says one word.

"S-s-shot."

My hands extend and grab the flashlight. I grab her shoulder with one hand and her head with the other as I roll her onto her back. As I run the beam all over her, looking for a bullet wound, I find nothing.

That's when my beam hits her thin veins, and I know that word has multiple meanings.

Shit. Shit! The insulin. She's in diabetic shock. A tremor runs through her body as she shrinks into a fetal position. Her body slows the shaking as she loses consciousness.

I kneel over the lady and check her pulse. It's slow. Like, crazy slow.

But it's there, and she's still alive. Somehow.

I turn the flashlight off and crouch over to the window, opening the heavy blinds. I don't see Riley outside, but that means nothing. He probably didn't see any light come from this room.

Maybe.

God, I hope not.

I sneak over to the bedroom door just as I hear the back door slam.

Sit-rep: I dropped the keys to the VW bug somewhere in the bedroom. I can grab them, but the garage door is still stuck. I can take off and, when I get somewhere, I can get the police to help. That might take, like, an hour. But the lady doesn't have an hour. She has minutes.

As I slowly close the bedroom door behind me and enter hallway, I grab the top lock from the floor where I left it, put it back in place on the door and clasp it shut.

Then I look for the top lock with my flashlight. It's only after I look all around the hallway and even in the child's bedroom does it hit me why I can't find it.

It's inside the room.

If Riley looks at this door and sees one lock is missing, I'm dead.

Then, as if the thought of this monster summoned him, I hear footsteps thunder from the living room.

"Rook?"

Riley calling my name jars me out of my fog.

"Um, I'm just finishing up in the bathroom."

As I take one step toward that door, my leg hits something sturdy and I let out a startled cry.

I don't have to angle the flashlight to know what just bruised my right shin: the heavy duty can opener. As I stare at it, I think about how I've been trying to find something the size of a mouse when I've got a damn loaf-of-bread-sized problem right here.

"Are you okay?" Riley's hurried voice matches quick stomps on the plush carpet.

I grab the can opener and fling it into the kid's room. It arcs through the air and lands on the edge of the twin bed.

Unfortunately, Riley will still get into the hallway before I can get to the bathroom.

With no rational choice, I make an irrational one. I turn my head back to the locked door, move my temple over the hinge for the top lock, and press my right temple against its jagged edge.

I push my head as hard as I can against the sharpest edge.

And then I twist.

My skin burns and tears at the same time. Every part of my body wants to scream, but I've already let one out in shock. When you cry wolf, you can't scream twice.

I crouch just as Riley rounds the corner and enters the hallway.

"Rook? Rook!"

I don't look up at him as he crouches and shines his flashlight on my downed head. Hopefully, he'll see the tear on my head, and not the carpet I'm bunching between my fingers.

"Hey, hey, are you okay?"

As the blood trickles from my temple to my chin, I groan. "I tripped over this damn old-ass carpet and hit my damn head on the damn door."

Through slit eyes, Riley's light goes first to my collected pile of carpet, then to the door. My back is against the bottom hinge, so Riley can't see that its lock is missing.

I lean my head up and smile. "I'm as graceful as a drunk bear."

"Ha, it's probably not that bad." Our eyes meet as Riley turns my head with one hand and holds the flashlight's beam on me, then lowers it. "You probably won't even need stitches, but it might leave a scar."

"Can't have a rainbow without the rain, can we?"

As we laugh, Riley moves his hand under my chin. For a second, I think he's going to try to kiss me again. Then a look crosses Riley's face. As his eyes run along the locked door behind me, he chews the inside of his cheek.

He's going to ask me if I tried to get inside that room. I just know it.

Then he swivels his head toward the kid's room.

Oh, shit, don't look in there. If he sees the can opener teetering on the edge of the bed, he might wonder why it's there.

I take my fingernail and dig it into my wound so it bleeds more. A small stream of blood flows out down to Riley's hand. Instinctively, he jerks it away and wipes the blood on the dirty carpet.

"Let's get you patched up." He pats my cheek and heads to the bathroom. "I'm gonna piss, then I'll find a first aid kit."

"'k."

A thud of a limb hitting the roof scares me, but not for the obvious reasons. I tilt my head toward the kid's room. The damn can opener shifts, with more of its weight angling toward the floor.

When Riley reaches the door, he turns back. I catch his gaze as he smiles.

"Hang in there, kid."

I smile and he shuts the bathroom door behind him. No, slams it. Without thinking, I dive sideways into the child's room. The thump I make is minimal compared to the thud the appliance would've made. I catch the falling can opener before it crashes onto the floor. Or more like it slips through my bloody hands and smashes into my chest. The wind abandons my body like someone just yelled *po-po* at a party. Yet I cannot scream.

It's times like these I remember that yelling and screaming won't fix a damn thing.

Chapter Thirty-Eight

Schnikt

THEN

Sit-Rep: Got my licenses. I need keys and an exit strategy. The front door is nine steps away. Too obvious. Back door is seventeen steps. Too much time to get there. The bathroom is my best bet. I can stand on the sink, pry open the window, and slide out. I just have to get Riley's keys first.

"You go to the Ship this year?" asks Stalin.

"Naw," answers the sheriff, "though I did listen to it on the radio."

"What's the Ship?" I ask, clearly out of some kind of loop.

"High school football championship." Riley scoffs. "Like there's any skill in football."

"And just how many times were you cut from the team, Cooter?" asks Stalin.

"I notice y'all didn't win the Ship, so maybe I could've helped."

"How?" Stalin throws his arms wide. "You can't run, catch, tackle, or kick."

"I'm good for morale."

"Whose?" Stalin chuckles. "If you can't do any of those, the only morale you're raising is the other team's!"

"Screw you, Battleship."

Stalin ignores Riley and continues. "Man, we had the perfect team. We were set to make a run for that trophy, Sheriff." Stalin shuffles the cards, even though we're not playing right now. I bet it's the same coping mechanism he uses when he dries a clean glass. "You ever think about that?"

"Only every day." The sheriff takes a puff of his pipe, and the smell of sweet tobacco and barley lingers in the air. "Cathedral had a real chance in the Ship this year. I mean, West played his heart out at QB. They were down, what, one touchdown going into the fourth?"

"Two," corrects Stalin.

"Right." The sheriff takes a swig. "That 80-yard drive and completed two-point conversion set them up to win with a TD. They even got the ball back and then..."

"Then the fumble."

"Right." The sheriff checks his watch, then sips his beer. "Just like in life, all it takes is one mistake for everything to come crashing down."

"If only we'd beaten Vardaman, then we'd have easily taken out Mantachie, and who knows where we would've wound up." Stalin stops shuffling, slides back in his chair, and takes a swig of beer. "Man, we could've been something."

"Yeah, we could've..." the sheriff just lets the awkwardness of this moment of childhood sports obsession hang in the air. While two grown men and a man-child stare at the table, I realize the real truth of the moment.

I'm stuck without a ride at the saddest boys' club in existence.

The window closest to me rattles and a sliver of moonlight slides in.

My inhibitions still pretty low, I point at the sheriff's lone Isotoner black leather glove on his right hand. "So, why are you like a white Michael Jackson?"

The sheriff sizes me up with his beady eyes, then yanks off the glove. Underneath it, I see a scarred hand with patchwork skin connected by thin scar lines. As he makes a fist, his hand makes a creaking sound like old leather desperate for oil.

"Jesus Christ..." I couldn't help myself; the words ejected from my throat before I could stop them.

"Was crucified, dead, and buried," adds Stalin.

The sheriff looks not at me, but Riley. There is some hidden stand-off, because Riley nods, and the sheriff begins.

"I was once a volunteer fireman. Years ago. Someone over on Hill-crest left a burner on. Next thing you know, the whole house is ablaze."

The sheriff takes out his zippo and *schnikts* it open and closed.

"I was first on the scene, so I was following protocol. I was on the radio with dispatch, giving them the details. Visible smoke, flames, but no one appeared in the structure. Downstairs was in flames, upstairs was billowing smoke. There was a lattice on the side of the house that could be used as a make-shift ladder, but the truck was fifteen minutes out, so I was ordered to wait. Plus, I had a buddy at the station bringing my gear with the truck."

The sheriff stops, swigs his beer, and flips his lighter.

Schnikt.

Schnikt.

Schnikt.

"And that's when I heard the screams."

A crash of a tree or large limb falling outside catches everyone off guard.

"The family was on the second floor. They could've jumped, but I guess that when they saw me, they thought that the firetruck was nearby and were waiting. I yelled for them to jump. There were four of them. Mother, father, a toddler, and a baby."

Riley reaches over and takes a swig from the tequila jug unprompted.

"The mother started out with the baby in her arms. She started walking on the roof, even though I told them to move to another window and jump. I told them to jump, dammit."

The sheriff holds his scarred hand up to the light. To me, it looks like something straight out of Frankenstein or a zombie movie like *Dawn of the Dead.*

"The fire was cooking the first floor, so naturally the roof was melting away. As one shingle caved in under her foot, the mother's leg went under, and—and she dropped the baby."

In that moment, the wind outside stops. There isn't even any ice pelting the tin roof right now. No one at the table shifts their weight, so there's not even a creak from a chair in the air.

"And the boy, well, he tried to dive from the window and grab the baby. I mean, he tried, but wound up rolling off as well."

Schnikt.

Schnikt.

Schnikt.

"And that's when I had to make a choice: catch the boy or catch the baby."

The sleet slams into the window behind me. Even so, I don't turn my gaze from the sheriff.

Into the silence, Riley adds a piece to this puzzle. "You made the wrong choice."

That's when it hits me square in the gut: Riley was the boy. This explains his rage toward the sheriff. What is it called, victim regret? No, it is survivor's guilt, where the living often hates their saviors and sometimes envy the dead.

Right now, a large piece of me relates to Riley, because neither of us should be alive today.

As I ponder about this story, these two men forever linked by one choice, Riley's eyes burn holes in the sheriff's skull.

"It was the unpopular decision, sure. What kind of monster would let a baby fall?" The sheriff rubs his gloved hand as he stares at the ceiling. "I, look, it wasn't like I was closer to the boy than the baby. I just made a call. Knowing what I know now, well Riley, you're right. Knowing what you've...wasted... I would've taken the baby and let the boy die from his own stupidity."

At this, Riley flips the poker table and charges. The sheriff never leaves his seat, sending an uppercut into Riley's jaw, taking the fight out of Riley and dropping him to his knees. The sheriff stands, grabs Riley by the shirt, and tosses him into the bathroom...which is exactly where I need to be.

"Throw some water on your face and man up." By the time the sheriff returns, Stalin and I have righted the table and are putting empty bottles in the trash. Unfortunately, the top was on the shitty tequila, so none of it poured out. The bottle might even be indestructible because there's not a scratch on it.

"So, I caught the boy. Then the roof slid on us. I put up this hand, and, well, let's say the fire got to it before I could get the two of us safely away."

The sheriff holds his hand out and shows me the palm. In it, is an indentation.

"That's from the hot nails stabbing my hand. To repair it, doctors took the skin from both of my butt cheeks."

"Wow." The lone word is not near enough to emphasize what the sheriff did. "Did—did anyone else make it out?" I venture.

"Oh, yeah." The sheriff puts back on his glove and continues. "The wife had burns like me, but the husband and wife made it. The baby lived fourteen days after the fall."

"But you saved the boy..."

"Well, that's done society a lot of good..." The sheriff checks his watch, then looks at his radio and adjusts a knob. "I guess you can live like a sinner as long as you die like a saint."

Riley returns from the bathroom, reaches over, and grabs the cards from in front of Stalin like nothing happened a minute ago. Upon closer inspection, there's a bit of white residue under his right nostril. Riley shuffles the deck. The sheriff cuts. When he does, the sheriff splits it away from the dealer. Apparently, Riley knows that is an insult, because he stares at the split deck and shakes his head.

"You gonna deal or not, Riley?" asks the sheriff, damn well aware of whatever drugs Riley snorted.

"Hold your horsies..." Riley reaches into his pocket, grabs a pill bottle, and snags a green-colored pill. He puts it on a playing card, smashes the pill with his beer bottle, then raises the card to his nose and snorts it.

"You just gonna do that in front of Sheriff?" Stalin asks.

"Ah, Cooter knows I'm not into pills no more." The sheriff leans across the table, picks up the bottle, and reads the label through a squint. "I've accepted my pain..."

The sheriff either needs reading glasses or is near-sighted.

"Riley's just being dramatic." The sheriff places the bottle back down. "Plus, he's got a prescription, and it ain't my job to complain about how he takes it. He could shove 'em straight up his ass if he liked."

Riley laughs, then he scans the room, thinking. "Would that make them more, um, potent?"

I cover my face to hide my smile. "Definitely."

"I concur," adds Stalin. Our eyes meet and we break our gaze before inevitable laughter gives us away.

Riley nods to himself and mumbles, "Okay, next time, next time."

I don't think we've even played a hand in the last few minutes. If we have, I probably lost. That must be why my tongue tastes like it licked a hot coal. Time is at a stand-still. The horrible liquor in my body makes me feel like I have the flu. Everything is wavy, and it covers the world in a mind-numbing haze.

A loud thump from the roof turns all of our attention. Then a second. A third. Next, a scratching like nails on a chalkboard forces everyone to cover their ears.

When it stops, Riley asks, "So, should we just get under the tables like we did in school every time we had a nuke attack drill?"

At this, the sheriff coughs while laughing, sending a plume of pipe smoke into the air. "Did you really think hiding under your desk would save you from a nuke?"

"Well, no, but maybe." Riley rubs his chin and squints at the sheriff. "Why? What do you think it was for?"

"You know how schools have assigned seats?" The cop leans back in his chair as we all nod. "So, the reason the government taught Cold War kids to hide under desks was so that a class roll book or district roll book or whatever could identify the dead."

"It was never about saving lives." Stalin sums up. "It was about inventory."

I guess because we were talking about school, I put my hand up to be called on. The sheriff chuckles and points at me with his pipe.

"Wouldn't the book just burn up in the blast?"

The sheriff's laugh starts low, then rises to a high pitch. He literally slaps his leg as he shakes his head. "That's our government for ya. Having half a thought and a tenth of the execution."

"Speaking of execution, you ever gonna deal, Cooter?" asks Stalin.

"Shut up, Battleship."

"Hey, if you're scared, say you're scared." Stalin's country accent makes the word *scared* sound more like *skeered*, but a taunt is a taunt.

"Why do you call him Cooter?" I ask. It's been bugging me for the last hour.

"Because all the girls in high school thought he had cooties." The sheriff answers the question so quickly he could be on a gameshow.

"I thought it was because that's a type of turtle and Riley here was a chubby kid with a fat head and used to get his head stuck like a turtle when he put on shirts," counters Stalin.

"Screw all of y'all," says Riley, unfolding his arms and flipping everyone off.

"Now, come on Riley, that's not fair." I put on my best damsel-in-distress voice as I lean in and place my hand on his thigh. "I'm new here. Surely you can't blame me?"

Riley's posture relaxes a bit. I run my finger down his cheek, but I'm still too far away to unclip the key from his belt without being obvious about it.

He sighs and says, "I just don't know why some bitches won't let me hit it."

"The phrases *bitches* and *hit it* are not helping your case."

"Naw, that's not it." Riley slides a bit away from me. "Probably because most of them are lesbians. Otherwise, they'd want some of deez nuts."

"You just ooze charm, Riley," Stalin grumbles.

"You know about that stuff, right?" Riley says, leaning toward Stalin. "Because you're so..."

"The word you're looking for is *fabulous*." Stalin gives up on Riley and grabs his cards. "Well, it's not like all of us fabulous types communicate—ow, dammit..."

Stalin's eyes light up—the sheriff clearly has kicked him under the table. The two exchange a glance and nod before Stalin continues.

"Uh, yeah, you're right on, Riley. They recruited a friend of mine, just last year. I think it was at, uh..."

Riley jumps in. "One of the Indiglo Girls concerts!"

"Sure."

"I knew it!"

The sheriff and I exchange mischievous looks. I jump on this bandwagon, if for no other reason than to get those keys.

I scoot toward Riley. "I'm sure they are. You're a catch." Despite my superb acting, I do almost throw up in my mouth. "You could've seen the signs."

"Wait, there are signs?" Riley shifts in his seat, not enough to move away, but enough that he is paying too much attention to me. "What are they?"

Stalin deals the cards as he says, "Well, here's what you need to know to avoid future confusion. As a proud member of the gay community, I think I can help you use your masculine skills to the best of your ability."

The sheriff looks at his new hand and adds, "And, as someone who has worked with all types of women, I would love to add to this discussion."

I glance at my shitty cards and toss three back. "And, as the lone set of ovaries among these brovaries, I should definitely contribute."

"I'll allow all of it." Stalin looks at his own cards and tosses one in. "First, Riley, avoid a woman whose hair is down to her butt.

The sheriff takes three cards. "And some whose hair is shorter, especially in the summer months."

"Good point. Secondly, if they like music, any music, don't bother."

"All music?" Riley tosses all his cards in for a new hand.

"Good catch," I add, as Stalin tosses me another handful of shit. "There's a huge chance that this girl will not be interested in your type if she can hear. Or see. Or smell."

"Wait, what?" Riley's eyes meet mine and I fake a cough to stifle a laugh and collect myself. With my cool under control, I pat Riley on the back.

"Never mind her," Stalin says. 'Finally, if they like animals, they won't like you."

"Should I be writing this down?"

"Oh, no, you'll be fine," I say as I rub his neck and use my other hand to unclip his keys from the belt. "Just remember, if a girl has any type of hair, likes any type of music, or likes any type of animal, you should just consider her a lesbian and leave her alone."

"Damn," mutters Riley as he rubs his chin. "Dating is hard."

Stalin pours us all a shot of straight tequila. "Well, we're glad to be of help to you and the community, Riley. To Riley!"

I'm too lit to argue. "To Riley," we all say.

I gag as the thick liquid covers my throat like a generic cough syrup. Honestly, I miss the hot sauce. At least it might cut the flavor of this shit.

"Y'all want to play for some real money?" asks Riley, his words stumbling over each other.

"You do realize you've lost almost every hand?" The sheriff asks.

Is Riley playing us? *What if this is all an act?*

I shake the notion from my head. He's not an evil genius; he's just a self-destructive asshole. It takes one to know one.

Sit Rep: Now all I have to do is get to the bathroom and I'm home free.

Chapter Thirty-Nine

Save a Dying Lady

NOW

"Ow, dammit, who taught you first aid, Freddy Krueger?"

Riley apparently thought it was *helpful* to douse the right side of my head in rubbing alcohol. As he does more harm than good, I regret not moving from the hallway into the living room when I had the chance.

"Thank goodness you've got me here because we gotta stop the bleeding..." Riley dabs a cotton ball on the wound and continues to teach me about stuff I know way better than him. "Enough alcohol will drown anything."

"One, that's wrong." I jam my hand into the clear plastic bag of cotton balls he brought from the bathroom's first aid kit and grab one. "Alcohol is to disinfect a wound as much as it is to stop bleeding. And two, it's pressure that closes a cut."

"I like what I said better."

Riley flips over my hands as he wipes blood from them. He stares at the two rough scars on my wrists. Even though I'm fairly light-skinned, the scars are brighter than my wrists. The one on my right wrist is fairly straight across, a single line from left to right. The left wrist's scar tissue is jagged, zigzagging like it was a scared chicken that kept second guessing if it would make it across the road.

"I didn't take you for a quitter."

I let him think his dark thoughts before responding.

"Riley, don't act like you know me or what I've been through."

"I'm just saying."

"And I'm not listening." I yank my wrists away. "Not about this."

A couple of light thuds hit the roof. Must be more falling limbs. I'm almost used to their sounds. I'm sitting cross-legged with my back still against the door. Riley splays out on the floor, legs wide like he's the world's least likely Calvin Klein model.

"What you said about alcohol was like it was a line straight out of a Merle Haggard song."

"Huh." Riley sits back, his eyes rolling back in his head, and sings a twangy, "Enough alcohol will drown anything."

He overemphasizes each syllable, the way an actor would in a made-for-TV movie about the South. I can just picture it: coming soon to ABC, *Humidity Stupidity: The Cooter Story.*

I can't let this innocuous moment fool me: this is still the guy who is holding a woman hostage. An elderly one who needs her insulin. I need to get Riley outside, or at least as far from the kitchen as possible.

Think, Rook, think.

It's not a flash of brilliance that hits me between the eyes. More of a flicker of lesser stupidity.

"Riley, I think my cut is going to need stitches."

"Well, the roads to the hospital are going to be tough."

"Hold up." I put my hand on his shoulder and give it a slight squeeze. "Weren't there some fishing polls in the shed in the back-yard?"

"So, you looked really good in there?" Riley's eyes widen and he swallows hard, as if he just got caught peeping in the girl's bathroom.

"Not really." That's not much of a lie, but this is. "If there are fishing polls, that's gotta mean that there is fishing line. Please-please-please go in there and find some. Now, it's gotta be thin. Think sewing-thread thin. Or spiderweb thin."

"Huh." Riley rubs his chin and narrows his stare at me. "Do they make it that thin?"

Hell if I know. "Yes, because some fish can see the thicker lines in the water."

"Okay, that makes sense." Riley grabs his flashlight and extends a hand to me.

I take it and he pulls me up, glancing down at the bedroom door behind me.

He looks at me with a blank stare and storms out without another word.

Shit. Did he just notice the bottom lock was missing?

"Hey, Riley, hold up..." I jog out of the hallway.

"Yeah." He never turns to face me as he approaches the back door. I get next to him just as he opens it. The icy blast of air in doesn't bother me as much as it did before, probably because the temperature in the house is dropping so fast. Even now, when Riley speaks, a small puff of visible air hangs between us.

"I just want to say thank you for taking me in and taking care of me." He turns, and I put my hand in the center of his chest.

"You didn't have to take me in. I know that I'm a stranger to you, and you know the night I've—we've—had and with this weather..." My words slur. *Get your shit together, girl.* "Look, all I'm saying is thank you."

"Rook..." Riley places his hand on mine. He squeezes it, a little harder than a caring touch, but not hard enough for me to cry out in pain.

"Yes."

Before he speaks, I already know what needs to happen. There is no time for any other option.

A fear-driven sweat drips into my head wound, stinging it enough to keep me in the moment. I sneak my left foot behind Riley's right foot and move all my weight to it. This is going to have happen in one move. Anything else, and he's got me.

Wait for it, Rook.

"What happened to the bottom lo—?"

Before he finishes asking, I hook the top of my left foot into the backside of Riley's right knee and I shove Riley to the right.

His uneven body swivels as he falls. Even disoriented, Riley grabs my hand. I catch myself on the door frame with my free hand and yank free of his grip.

Before Riley even hits the ground outside, I've grabbed the doorknob. By the time he's up, I've shut and locked the door. And by the time he's slamming his shoulder into it, I've got a chair under the doorknob. It won't hold for long, but it's all I've got.

Now to save a dying lady without becoming one myself.

Chapter Forty

A Knife's Cold Blade

NOW

I leave the kitchen and dart to the front door. I lock it and put a chair under the doorknob. I have mere minutes until Riley tries smashing any of the many windows along the cabin's perimeter. Back in the kitchen, I fling the fridge's door wide open and grab the bottle of insulin.

"Needle, needle, needle," I chat to myself as I look through the fridge for it. Then I shake that stupid notion that someone would store a hypodermic needle in a fridge.

I check the drawer next to the fridge. Among the expired coupons, rubber bands, and ketchup packets is a leather pouch about the size of a paperback book. I know it too well, so I grab it and sprint to the bedroom. That's when my hearing tells me something it shouldn't.

Riley has stopped pounding.

He is about to find another way in.

Or he may even already be in the cabin.

Approaching the door, I don't even slow down, tucking my shoulder, and slamming into the bedroom door. I don't have time to finagle the lock with the magnet this time. Riley will be in here at any second.

Unfortunately, someone made the door out of the stuff of Captain America's shield and everything in my body screams out in pain as I crash to the floor.

As I pick myself off the shitty rug, I don't even take a beat to curse myself for being lazy. Instead, I grab the electric can opener from under the kid's bed and slam the magnet into the lock.

With a *schlack*, the magnet pops loose.

Once inside, I turn on the light so that I can see the lady. A huge part of me hopes she will sit up because the light is assaulting her eyes.

Instead, she lays there like a corpse.

I unzip the pouch. Inside is a syringe and three metal needles. I grab the first and screw it onto the syringe. In ideal situations, I'd inject insulin at room temperature. Plus, I should check to see if it's expired.

The dying don't get ideal situations.

I tear off the plastic cover of the bottle. Next, I take the glass cap off the metal needle. I pull back on the plunger to put air in the syringe. Then I put the needle into the bottle, and push all the air in.

Something hits the window and I drop everything, startled. There's nothing there, so I pick up the needle-and-bottle combo. I blow out the last bit of air into the bottle. Holding the bottle upside down, I keep the needle in the liquid's bottom to keep any oxygen from getting in. I pull out the needle at the right dosage level and push the plunger in the air so that a trickle of insulin arches in the air.

Finding no bubbles in the syringe, I roll up the lady's arm. Her recessed veins, probably from malnourishment and dehydration, rule out anything in the arms.

So I go to the tops of the feet. The lady's right foot doesn't have a single vein I can use. It might as well be a mannequin's leg.

Wait. Insulin goes into fatty tissue, not the bloodstream. I knew this, I'm just rattled.

I go to her left thigh and angle the tip of the needle so that it will slip right under her paper-thin skin. The needle breaks the skin, plunges into the thigh, and I push the insulin in.

Nothing happens. I can't even tell if the lady's still breathing. I try to find a pulse, but her clammy skin bunches under my sweaty hands.

As I put my ear to her chest, I listen. Nothing.

I'm too late.

But I have to try.

I put my hands on top of her sternum and push.

As if on cue, a log smashes through the bedroom window.

Riley is coming.

After I jump off the lady, I dart into the bathroom, looking for something, anything, to save our lives.

That's when I find my weapons.

The crinkle of glass being raked away with something tells me Riley is clearing the windowsill before he enters. I yank back the curtain and blast him in the face with *Hold it with Final Net* hairspray. The spray cloud of permahold is so thick even I choke on it.

Riley screams out and claws at his eyes as I kick him in the chest, right back through the window. He falls backward and scampers away, still cursing and trying to pull the gunk from his face.

I don't know how much time I just bought us, but I've got to use every second.

Stepping back, though, an icy hand covers my mouth and a knife's cold blade touches my neck.

Chapter Forty-One

Asking the Wrong Questions

THEN

The storm rages as Riley reaches into his jeans and pulls out a gold pocket watch. It dangles from a chain as he makes an *oooohhh*sound and sways the watch side to side.

"Let me see that." The sheriff reaches for it.

Just before he grabs it, Riley yanks it back. "Psych! Not yours unless you win it."

"Cooter, you been robbing houses?" Stalin's question has a heaviness to it, like he really wanted to add the word *again* to that sentence.

"Nope." Riley winds the watch and holds it to his ear. "Got this for services rendered."

"People don't pay plumbers with gold, Riley," The sheriff says, clearly a little ticked.

"First of all, I'm not a plumber. I'm an installer. Get it right." Riley points to a certificate above the bar. "Secondly, I want to play for that damn MacGuffin."

Since I have zero idea what the hell a MacGuffin is, I follow Riley's finger.

"The top shelf vodka?" I ask.

"Nope." Riley smiles. "The certificate."

"Go to hell." Stalin gathers up the cards and stomps away.

Even I know what the document is. Especially because I needed to cash one of them in.

A life insurance bond.

"What?" Riley leans back in his chair with arms wide enough to look like an evangelist on Sunday. "You're never gonna cash it in."

"And you're never gonna earn it, let alone win it. Tell you what, you find my mama, it's all yours."

"No body, no bounty," the sheriff reminds Riley.

Stalin nods slowly, as if his head is anchored to the floor.

Riley flicks the watch with his thumb and middle finger, spinning it. "Well, sheriff, I'll bet this against any gold you've got."

At that taunt, the sheriff touches his wedding ring. "What I have, I'm not willing to risk."

"It's not like it means anything anymore."

The sheriff bites the inside of his cheek and leaves the table.

Whatever this is about is none of my business.

"I need to see a garden about some watering," I say, getting up from the table, stumbling a little on my jelly legs. Luckily, it is a forward stumble.

Entering the bathroom, I shield my eyes. I forgot about the damn red-light lava lamp strobing effect in here.

After I spot the toilet, I understand why. The nastiest shitter I've seen since Mister Three Steps played a rainy *Sister Wife* festival in Osceola, Arkansas, to a crowd of drunk schoolteachers. I've seen frat guys, law students, and even underage kids drink less than teachers that just got out for summer.

The red light covers up the black stains on the side of the bowl. The water itself looks dark, and after I flush it only a trickle comes back in. A moaning in the wall next to the window tells me the temperature is dropping below twenty degrees. I bet this bar isn't insulated worth a damn, so it is only a matter of time before the pipes burst.

Not like I'll be here when it happens.

I stand on the sink and grab the lock to the window and pull it down. The lock comes loose a bit, but the window only budges enough to let the cold air in and not me out. Damn thing is frozen from the outside.

Having grown up mostly in Michigan, I know all it takes to make a homemade de-icer is soap, alcohol, and water. I can pour the contents down the window's edges through the crack and it will quickly thaw.

Two of the three ingredients are in this bathroom. All I have to do is get that jug of tequila, and I'm out.

Just before I step down, I spot movement through the fogged-up glass. After rubbing a clear spot with my sleeve, I can't see it anywhere.

I'm more drunk than I thought.

I hop down and collect my thoughts as I exit the bathroom.

Sit-Rep: The sheriff is in front of the bar. He's two steps from my direct path but facing my way. I can't get the jug from the table or any liquor from behind the bar. Riley is near the back door, patting down his pockets. He's about to look for his keys. Stalin is at the front door, watching the storm.

I need one good distraction to get the sheriff looking away. As I glance over the bar, I notice a black-and-white picture of a young woman holding something. As I step closer, I notice it is a toddler.

"Stalin, is that your mother?" I ask, knowing damn well it is, but hoping he's drunk enough to run me through it again.

"Sure is." Stalin walks behind the bar and takes the black frame from the wall. He hands it to me. In the photo, a blond woman smiles while she looks at the kid. The child's chubby fingers play with a heart-shaped necklace that dangles from his mother's neck.

"She's lovely."

"She was."

The weight of the word *was* lowers the bartender's shoulders. He breaks eye contact with me and starts a drip on the faucet.

"Anyone seen my keys?" asks Riley from under our poker table.

"They're probably with your tooth," quips the sheriff. His radio squawks and he steps to the back of the room.

"I bet they fell out when you were looking for some shooting liquor."

Riley nods and darts behind the bar. My lie is a quick fix. I have maybe a minute before Riley goes from asking the wrong questions to asking the right ones.

With no eyes on me, I grab my bass guitar from the stage and the tequila from the table, and dart back into the bathroom.

Chapter Forty-Two

Away

NOW

"Who the hell are you?" The lady's breath reeks of bile and funk, like the last time she brushed her teeth Richard Nixon was president. My every instinct is to jam my hand into the knife's blade, protecting my throat but slitting open my palm.

Sit-Rep: The belief of the lady's demise is greatly exaggerated, and now she has a knife to my throat. She's likely not a killer, otherwise my shirt would be stained crimson. However, there's a good chance she's out of her mind. Riley's location is unknown. Rook, slow down and talk to her. Even though Riley is outside and has access to the ax and probably every other weapon in that shed.

"I'm, um, a friend."

This exaggeration is about as nice a way as I can say *hi, I broke into your house and ate your food but I did bring you back to life so please don't kill me.*

"I don't have any friends of your persuasion."

Some people just say *black,* but whatever floats her boat.

"That's because, I'm, um..." Think, Rook, think. "I'm a friend of your son's."

Please-don't-be-a-dead-kid.

"You know Bobby?" The blade on my neck loosens, and I almost say *yes*, just out of sheer joy of not getting my throat slit. However, just before I say anything, my mind jumps back to the kid's bedroom and the name on the dresser.

This is a test. "I don't know who *Bobby* is, but I know Carolton."

Then, just as quickly as the knife was at my throat, it drops, though the phantom blade still nicks at my neck.

"That'll do, girlie." The lady steps in front of me. She turns the knife around and around in her hand before she asks her next question. "So, where's Carolton?"

"Out." This question isn't one I think I can bluff, so I ask, "Where did you think he'd be?"

"I thought he'd be here checking on his dear ole mum, but he's an ungrateful little bastard. He's probably holing up with some two-bit floozie who dresses like a whore." She points the knife blade at my body and runs it up and down. "No offense."

"Hey, you're the one wearing only a nightgown."

Just as I think that might have been a step too far, she smiles like a jackal.

"I like you. You've got spunk." Then she points the knife blade at the window. "Did you do that?"

"Shit!" When someone jams a knife to your neck, you lose track of the maniac outside. "We've got to go."

"Go where?"

I grab her thin wrist and head to the garage. "Away."

Chapter Forty-Three

Fear Anchors My Feet

THEN

I dash to the bathroom. Once inside, I anchor my bass guitar between the doorknob and floorboards. It's a crude doorstop, but it will hold a few seconds if anyone tries to come in.

I grab the generic soap dispenser off the edge of the sink and pour yellow liquid soap into the jug and turn on the faucet. The pipes shriek. A trickle of water gets thinner and thinner until a gush of water explodes all over the sink.

Then the water stops completely.

Shit. I'm too drunk to remember the proportions for this homemade de-icer, but I don't think I have enough water.

It is what it is now.

With no other choice, I put the lid on the jug and shake it like my life depends on it.

"Hey, Rook, are you okay in there?" asks Stalin knocking on the door, the concern in his voice almost fatherly.

"Yeah." *Damnation*. That pipe did sound like a scream. Through winded gasps, I say, "It's just the pipes."

"It's okay if you throw up. There's no shame in calling some dinosaurs."

"I'm fine. Just give me a minute."

Trying to move quickly, I haphazardly put one foot on the sink and rise on the wet edge of the sink. My shoe slips and the jug escapes my grip, hitting top-down on the wood, breaking off at the top, and sloshing onto the ground.

"Shit!" I fumble for the jug, righting the bottom part just enough to save it. Ultimately, I wind up with a split jug with more de-icer in the bottom, so I take the larger part.

Though I might need every bit to get out of here.

The jagged edge slices the palm of my right hand just deep enough to bleed. Even so, I hold on to it and maneuver the sink as if I am walking a tightrope.

Once I get to the edge, I equally distribute the remaining de-icer onto the frozen hinges and say a prayer.

Ice crackles, telling me it's working.

I toss the glass in the plastic trashcan near me and grab my bass from under the door. With one hand, I open the window.

About time something goes right.

Then, just as I place my right foot on the sink, preparing to throw my bass through and follow it to freedom, I spot a man pacing in the parking lot.

I wouldn't have noticed him there if I didn't see the red cherry of a lit cigarette get brighter as he took a puff.

I wait until he gets past, then think I can make a run for it. Fear anchors my feet as I doubt myself.

What is he doing out in this storm?

Chapter Forty-Four

Rotary

NOW

We dash into the garage. I ask the lady, "Do you have a gun?"

"Not since my son took it away from me for shooting at the census man."

A no would've sufficed...

"The good news is I've hidden my emeralds in here, so no one can take them."

"That's good news, but great news includes getting out of here alive..."

"And don't you go stealing them, you hear?"

Racist old bat.

Without thinking, I pull on the garage door chain, but it's still stuck.

The lady squints at me. "What the hell are you—"

Grabbing the bottle of de-icer from the shelf, I put my finger over her lips to warn her. She knocks my hand away.

"Don't you shush me in my house, lil girl," she whispers. I live for small victories.

"Look, I'm going to sneak outside and de-ice the door. You stay put."

I move toward the door, and the lady grabs my shoulder. "I'm stronger than I look."

"You were dead two minutes ago."

"Were you born a smartass, or did you have to grow into it?"

I smile and give her hand a squeeze. "A little Column A, a little Column B."

"Well, I'm going to find a weapon or something..."

I leave the lady in the garage and renter the hallway. As I creep, the wind knocks limbs as they scratch against the windows. I don't know how long I have until Riley finds me.

Then, hanging on the wall in the kitchen, I see it. An old rotary landline phone. Rotary phones still work even when the power goes out.

I doubt anyone could get to us in this weather, but I have to try. I crouch and move toward the phone. As I get there and grab the phone off the hook, I listen for the wonderful sound of a dial tone.

The flat hum welcomes me. I loop my finger into the Nine slot and crank it clockwise. The ticks of notches echo in the silence. When I let go, the dial whirls quickly back into place.

Just as I hook my finger into the One slot and pull, the back door pops open.

"Where the hell are you?!"

The rage in Riley's voice adds to the cold, biting wind that fills the cabin. I push myself so hard into the side of the wall—so that Riley won't see me—that I mentally try to morph into it. As I do so, the One slot clicks the dial back.

I'm only one digit away, but I can't let Riley to find me.

I peek down and around the corner. I'm greeted by the back of Riley's boots.

He's right there...

I have maybe three seconds to hang up the phone before the disconnect squawk alerts Riley. On the other hand, if I put the receiver back on the holder, that *click* might get Riley's attention. My best bet is to pull as slowly as possible. I hook my fingernail into the slot and pull up on my nail, pinching uncomfortably until there is the slightest *tick* as I pull down. My spine, though I'm crouched, straightens. I grit my teeth so hard something in my jaw pops.

Now to move the One slot back to the standard setting and it'll call the police.

Riley's position has shifted. I now see the back of his boots, but they haven't moved away. He's surveying the Living Room and probably deciding what to do. My every instinct is to run, but I can't leave the lady. Riley has held her captive long enough.

The boots move away stomping thunder on the carpeted floor as Riley moves to the hallway.

I let go of the dial.

Tick. It might as well be a foghorn.

Riley stops mid-step.

I push my back against the wall as he angles the flashlight into the kitchen.

Oh-please-oh-please-oh-please...

He takes one step, then another. I cover the earpiece of the receiver as hard as I can. Even muffled, I hear the flat sound of my line ringing the emergency line.

The light grazes past my face. I don't think he can see me, but I can't be sure. I cradle the phone which may yet become an impromptu weapon.

The line keeps ringing. The storm has probably swamped the police with calls, but I've got to reach them.

Then the light moves away just as I hear the operator on the other end of the phone pick up.

"Hello, this is 911. What is your emergency?" The operator's voice stifled under my hand. I glance out and don't see Riley, so I put the phone up to my ear.

"Thank God you picked up," I whisper-yell into the phone. "There is a lady being held hostage and I'm trying to get us—"

The thud of the ax into the wall just above my head cuts the call off.

I scream and drop the receiver, getting tangled in the crazy-long phone cord, rolling around to try to get out and get away.

Riley is using two hands to pry the ax from the post.

"Did you call the damn police?" The ax head comes loose, so Riley shoves the handle back into the ax head and twists it free. "Are you out of your mind?"

I kick free of the cord and make a break for it. Riley grabs my shoulder and spins me to face him. The rage in his eyes practically burns me as he holds the ax blade near my face.

"We don't have to deal with the police, because we're only trespassing."

I knew this wasn't your cabin.

"Bullshit!" I shove him hard enough to spin us both, but Riley holds tight. "You've been keeping that lady hostage for I-don't-know-how-long."

He has a moment to look confused at that, but only a moment. In short order, confusion gives way to pain as he screams and drops the ax and his grip on me. Suddenly, a hot, warm wetness covers where my stomach connects with Riley's. I reach down and my fingers come away red and sticky.

As his eyes roll back into his head, Riley turns to the right where the lady stands with a very bloody knife with something on the handle that I can't quite make out.

Riley only has time to say one thing before losing consciousness and collapsing into my arms.

"Where the hell did you come from?"

Chapter Forty-Five

My Window

THEN

Get it together, Rook. I shake my head and scan the perimeter for the stranger, but he's out of sight already. Maybe he got in his car and left. If he parked on the side of the bar, I would never have heard him crank the engine over the sounds of the storm outside.

I chew my lip, wondering if it would be better to risk getting caught by a stranger outside than by the sheriff inside. I slide my bass through the opening, and with a heave, follow it through.

I'm home free!

Something grabs my dreads and pulls. "Come here!"

I scream, falling back onto the icy gravel. The follicles in his grasp burn, as if someone put a hot poker to my head. I'm now eye-level with a broad-shouldered man with straight black hair and a perfectly trimmed goatee. His bloodshot eyes and the stale stench of cheap bourbon on his breath tell me he's as out of it as Riley is.

He pins my arms to my body so I can't punch or scratch my way free.

"Why'd you break my window?" he demands as our noses touch.

"I di-di-didn't break anything! Ow-ow-ow!"

He rotates me to see that I snapped the right hinge after I got the bathroom window open.

What the hell does he mean my *window?*

"You're gonna pay for that."

I don't take the time to tell him to *put it on my tab*. Instead, I kick him square in the balls and dive back in through the window.

I crash down on the bits of broken glass from the busted tequila jug, but these papercuts are the least of my worries. The impact knocks the wind out of me. And the man breaks for the window himself, trying to fit through.

While my chest and throat battle over breathing dominance, the man slides back outside, rage in his pinkish eyes.

I should've paid more attention to the shotgun he is now holding.

Chapter Forty-Six

Nothing Steals Joy

NOW

"What the hell did you do?" I yell at the crazy lady. My hands jump to the wound to put pressure on it. I don't know what the lady punctured when she stabbed him, but Riley's out cold.

"Well, it looked to me that your friend there was about to *ax* you a question, as you kids say."

"You're not funny, especially when you're stabbing people." I glance around the room and spot Riley's bag. "We've got to get some Quik-Clot from Riley's B.O.B."

"Hun, none of the words you just said made a lick of sense."

"Just, shit, just put your hands right here."

I grab the lady's hands and she jerks away. "I'm not touching him. Hell, I don't even know him."

How can you not know your captor? I guess he kept her so drugged up or insulin-deprived that she's just been in a near-coma.

Ignoring her excuse, I counter, "Hey, you broke him, you bought him."

I'm pretty sure she calls me something less than flattering under her breath, but she reluctantly crouches and puts pressure on the wound.

I dart to Riley's B.O.B. which is still on the couch in the corner of the living room and quickly dump all the contents out onto the floor. I pop open the silver first aid kit, grab the sealed adhesive QuikClot, and tear it open with my teeth. When I crouch down next to Riley, the lady raises his shirt to reveal a gushing, one-inch wound. I yank off the adhesive side of the bandage and slam it on Riley. Even unconscious, he mumbles something in pain.

"Why would you want to save him?" asks the lady. Maybe she's in shock.

"I'm not a killer."

"In case you weren't paying attention, I'm the one who stabbed him."

"Well, at this point doing nothing is the same as killing him in my book."

I push along the seams of the bandage. It turns slightly pink, but no blood oozes out.

The lights flicker and I catch the lady looking me over from head to toe.

"Huh..." I don't know what to make of the lady's response to this.

There is a series of strobes, lights flickering almost rhythmically, as the power struggles to stay on. In the flashes, I can make out the details on the knife now on the ground. The blackish blade is now crimson. The handle has a figure on it that appears to be the happy chubby guy. *Dammit, what's his name? Ah, the Buddha.*

"My husband took this off one of them Jap-o-nese," says the lady, sensing my curiosity, "during the battle of Guadalcanal. Had to go hand-to-hand when his M1 jammed. Yanked this right off the little bastard's bayonet, then gave it right back to him, business-end first."

Is that a twinkle in the lady's eyes, or is it the flickering lights?

I check Riley's pulse. Steady. His breathing is slow yet consistent. It's almost like the lady hit a spot on his body that caused instant sleep.

Lucky us...

"Let's use the cut phone cord to tie him up."

"Girl, he's asleep."

"Aren't you just Captain Obvious?" I shove a handful of the cord into the lady's hands. "He's still dangerous."

As we roll Riley onto his stomach, he grunts in pain. I wait for him to jump up. Instead, he snores. As we move his hands behind his back and tie them with the cord, the lights cut on.

"Perfect."

The lady narrows her gaze on me.

I can't tell why, so I hop up and dust off the front of my pants. "I'm going to thaw the garage door and get us out of here."

"Who knows about him?" The lady asks as she paces. "I mean, besides the two of us."

"I don't know. I think that when I called 911, the call was...cut off." I grab the flask-sized de-icer bottle from where I dropped it and smile. "But it's about to be a whole bunch of people once we get to town."

The lady does not return the smile. Instead, she wipes each side of the bloody knife on Riley's jeans.

Whatever that is about, I won't take time to guess. I open the front door, and the wind slams into me, knocking me back into the cabin. Once braced, I lower my head and move out again.

Outside, I slip on the iced-over concrete. I don't fall, but I *am* glad no one saw me do an interpretive dance to save my literal ass.

Slow and steady, Rook.

I shove the de-icer under my shirt, then tuck the shirt's ends into my pants, freeing up both hands so can I walk this icy tight rope all the way to the garage.

Once there, I untuck my shirt and whip out the de-icer, starting at the top left corner of the garage door and working my way around, finishing at the bottom where the rim meets the concrete.

That should do it. I shake the plastic container. There are a few ounces left. *You never know when we'll need this.*

We might not freeze to death out in the middle of nowhere after all.

I tuck the de-icer back under my shirt and tuck in the corners.

As I open the front door and enter the living room, I internally celebrate.

We've stopped the bad guy.

We have power.

And now we can probably wait out the storm since Riley's bleeding is under control.

There is nothing that steals joy like a knife in the gut.

Chapter Forty-Seven

Shick-shack, Snick-clack

THEN

"Shit!" I scream and dart behind the stall, hoping that the rusted stainless metal barrier catches any buckshot or slug headed my way. I tense up and brace, but nothing happens. I lean over and catch my attacker in the bathroom mirror's reflection.

He sees me and aims the gun at the mirror, and I dart out the door and into the main bar.

"Gun!" I scream.

That one word is all it takes. Stalin drops his broom and dashes behind the bar. Riley grabs a decorative antique farming scythe from off the wall. And the sheriff moves for his revolver still in the basket.

However, none of them make it. The front door opens and the international sound for *halt* fills the air as our gunman racks his shotgun.

Shick-shack.

No one moves. I don't even breathe.

Sit-Rep: I'm two steps from the bathroom. I can still get out. That will draw the gunman's fire. However, he's forty-five degrees away. Depending on what he's loaded that shotgun with, he'll either miss me with a slug or tear out my side with buckshot. Riley is the closest to him but not within striking distance. He'll have to throw the scythe sheathe at the gunman, two motions at minimum, a backward pull and a forward heave. The sheriff is two steps from his revolver. Both he and Riley are in the gun's blast radius. Stalin is the farthest away but only has a baseball bat. Unless the big guy can hit the bullet back at the gunman, he's useless.

Time stands still as the gunman shuts the door without taking his eyes off us.

Then Stalin does the last thing I would do in this situation.

He starts laughing.

"Dammit, Dante, I put you on probation for whacking it in the bathroom, so you're not even supposed to be here today."

"Don't give me any of that bullshit, Stalin." The gunman stomps the wood floor, as if the shotgun wasn't enough of an attention-getter. "I need money."

"Clearly you don't, because that shotgun still has the price tag hanging from its trigger."

Sure enough, a dangily white tag on a piece of string sways under our gunman's trigger finger. Stalin puts down the bat and walks toward Dante. His pup, Cotton, sensing something, growls. Stalin waves the pup to *lay back down.*

"Stalin, you sure you want to do that?" Riley asks.

The sheriff takes a step closer to his revolver.

"Everybody, get back!" The gunman motions with the gun's barrel for us to move. "Get to the middle of the room! Move!"

Riley, the sheriff, and I all step to where Dante's shotgun implies. Only Stalin keeps moving toward him.

"Dante, if you just put the gun down and leave, we can talk about this in the morning. Clearly you're drunk—"

"You're damn right I'm drunk!" Spit flies from Dante's lips as his yell echoes in the room. Stalin slows his walk. "I had to get this way to get up the nerve."

"Well, just put the gun down and we'll worry about everything tomorrow."

Stalin's giant mitt touches the shotgun's barrel. For a second, I'm expecting him to drop the gun or for Stalin to yank it out of his hands.

Instead, he steps back, moves his trigger hand, and smacks Stalin across the face with the shotgun's wooden stock. Stalin stumbles back onto the floor.

"Sometimes I hate this damn bar," mumbles Stalin through bloody lips.

"Get over there with the rest of them!"

"Son, don't go doing anything foolish." The sheriff might mean well saying this, but at this juncture it is the same as telling someone to *calm down*.

"Shut up. You ain't the law." Dante spits in the sheriff's general direction. "You're just a pariah. I know what you done, Sheriff."

My curiosity is certainly piqued, though it's mildly dampened by the loaded gun waving about the room. I can't be distracted by history right now when the future is at stake.

The sheriff's silver lighter is on the table, etched with the words: *Let the bridges you burn light your way.*

Reading over those words, a Hail Mary option opens in my mind.

A gust of wind swings open the front door, distracting Dante and giving me a chance to dart back to the bathroom.

"Get back here!"

I slam the door shut and grab the last bit of de-icer left in the top of the broken bottle.

As Dante kicks the door in, I turn and douse him with the water-and-soap mixture.

And one-hundred-and-twenty proof tequila.

Dante throws up his hands, so it soaks his arms, chest, crotch, and one leg.

My window to act closing, I drop the jug and raise my weapon. The *schnikt* sound gets his attention because, just like the shotgun, it, too, is a universal sound.

"Drop the gun, or I drop this," I command, holding the red flame in front of his face.

"You don't seem like the type that would light a guy on fire, missy."

"I'm not, but gravity sure will."

I don't know if he does this on purpose, or if he is just nervous, but Dante racks the shotgun again. By doing this, an ejected shell should bounce on the floor.

It doesn't.

The gun is empty.

Then one final universal sound catches my attention.

The *snick-clack* of a revolver's hammer.

Chapter Forty-Eight

Green Eyes

NOW

I stare directly at my assailant. Nothing makes sense. I glance down. Just below my midsection is the Buddha knife inserted up to the hilt. The jolly fat man stares at me as stars flash before my eyes. Looking back up, I meet a smile full of not just mischief, but also joy.

"You damned green eyes." The lady's eyes sparkle with madness. "Never could trust a one of ya."

She pulls on the knife, but it catches.

A look of concern crosses her face as I jerk away. The good news, for me anyway, is that the knife's blade went straight into the thin plastic de-icer bottle I had tucked into my pants. The bad news is that she shoved the blade hard enough that it not only punctured both sides of the bottle, but also my left love handle.

And there's probably some de-icer in my bloodstream as well as the tip of the filthy knife.

Poisoning is the least of my current concerns.

As I tear at the knife, the lady shrieks and grabs a handful of my dreads, slamming me against the coffee table. When McStabby here said she was *stronger than she looks*, she wasn't kidding! My insides burn not just from the de-icer, but also the tearing of flesh and muscle.

Standing in front of the giant bookshelf, she raises the blade again. I don't think, kicking her square in the chest and sending her flying into the books. The shelf teeters, and this time the popping of wood comes from inside, not outside, of the house.

I roll the hell out of Dodge.

The lady isn't as lucky.

As the case crashes down, the only part of her that isn't covered is her right hand, still gripping the knife.

Run, Rook, run. Every fiber in my body screams this. Yet I must know if she's still alive. I check her pulse with one hand and prop the other next to her hand. This way I don't fall onto the bookshelf and cause any more damage to Jason Voorhees' mother.

Just when I think I find one, the blade of the knife swings and papercuts my hand.

"Damn old bitch!" I stand and kick the bookcase.

The lady moans, then screams. "Damn green eye!" She swipes at the air with her knife.

I dart to the bedroom and grab the keys to the VW bug. The lady will live until I get the police here.

Probably.

I head to the garage but, as I glance out of the hallway, I discover a new, terrifying problem.

Riley has escaped.

Chapter Forty-Nine

IT'S ALIVE

NOW

I shine the old flashlight around the kitchen and living room finding only the jumbled cords I used to hold Riley's arms behind his back. I check the kitchen, the bathroom, the kid's room, and even the lady's room.

He's gone.

In the living room, I notice the back door slightly ajar.

He's out.

Go, Rook, go.

I run to the garage and pull on the chain for the garage door. It raises an inch and the remaining ice on the door cracks, sounding like a bowl of Rice Krispies in milk. With two more heaves, I get the door all the way open.

The driver's side door of the yellow VW bug creaks loudly, begging for oil. Sitting behind the wheel of this relic from the 1960s, it occurs to me that old cars in cold weather have one thing in common.

They will only crank if they want to.

"Mr. Bug, please crank." Sure, it's farfetched that the car hears me, but at this point I will take it to prom and let it get to second base if it cranks. "I will not flood your engine when you turn over unless you want me to, okay?"

Thankfully, the car doesn't answer. However, considering the night I have had, I wouldn't be surprised if this car really was Bumblebee from the *Transformers* and came to life.

I insert the key and give it a slight turn. The lone *tick* the car makes confirms the battery is working. I turn the ignition over fully. The engine whirs and almost catches, like it doesn't know whether or not it wants to get out in this weather.

Me, too, Mr. Bug, me too.

I press the accelerator gently, like there is an egg I don't want to crack.

The motor fights to live but isn't turning over.

"Okay, Mr. Bug, one big push...please wake up..."

I squish the invisible egg as I floor the accelerator. Like Frankenstein's monster after getting hit with thousands of bolts of electricity, the engine roars to life.

"IT'S ALIVE!" I scream, quoting the movie's line correctly.

My win ices over when a bloody hand slaps against the passenger window.

Chapter Fifty

The Other Way

THEN

Sit-Rep: Dante's shotgun is empty. The sheriff's revolver is cocked. His view is blocked. He's about to shoot a man who is no more of a threat to me than the farting dog in the corner.

Without thinking more, I toss the lighter and catch Dante on fire. While it is my quickest choice, because I don't have time to yell to the sheriff that the gun wasn't loaded, it's probably not my kindest move.

It's also not my dumbest. The blue flame on his chest forces Dante to stumble and slam into the opposing wall. As he does so, I dive to the left. There is a roar of the blast, followed by the crack of a heated projectile whizzing past my left shoulder. The tile behind me explodes.

I pounce on Dante and extinguish the flames with a few palm slaps. The soap must've diluted the alcohol's flammability. Even so, Dante kicks me away.

"You caught me on fire!"

Dante lies on the ground, his grip firm on his shotgun, like Linus in *Peanuts* holding onto his blanket.

The sheriff's hard booted steps shake the floorboards.

"Toss the gun, asshole!" I yell at Dante, desperate for this to be over.

Dante then pushes it away as if spiders cover it.

Just then, the sheriff stands over Dante, gun aimed at his head.

"Sheriff, he's tossed the gun! Don't shoot! He's unarmed!"

The sheriff cocks the revolver again.

"He still looks armed to me." The sheriff lowers his gun to the knife on Dante's belt.

"Sheriff, wait." Dante's pleads. "*Everyone* carries a knife in the Delta."

"Plus, you heard him rack the gun a second time." I add. "No shell ejected. It's empty!"

"Couldn't hear that all the way over there." The raspiness in the sheriff's voice fits his stare.

Bullshit. It was so quiet at that moment you could've heard a mouse fart.

Dante is just drunk, not a killer. I have half a plan to get out of this. What I need is a miracle.

The sheriff's radio squawks. "Looking for anyone with a 10-28 about last communication. Over."

Even hearing the radio, the sheriff keeps his gun on Dante.

"Look, I'll just take it off," Dante offers.

Understanding pierces my thick skull. The sheriff needs Dante to be holding the knife to justify killing him.

Moving at lightspeed, I yank the knife out and toss it out of the bathroom.

The look that crosses the sheriff's face starts as rage, but slowly morphs to acceptance. Whatever demon in the sheriff's blood that is craving a kill will have to find it some other day.

The sheriff lowers the gun's hammer and holsters his revolver. He snatches a wad of plastic zip ties from his belt and flings them at me. I catch them but not before they smack my right ear, sending a sharp pain up the side of my head.

"Zip him; I'll be back."

The sheriff grabs his radio and leaves the bathroom.

With a moment to breathe, I look over Dante. The room smells of burnt hair and shit. His skin is a shade darker than it was, but with some aloe it won't be worse than a solid sunburn. Finally, he holds his sweatshirt that appears to have a burned-out local mascot of either a cat, horse, or soldier on it. I can't remember what it was before I went all bananas foster on him.

"Girl, you ruined my hoodie!" he peels a large chunk off and tosses it at me. "It was vintage."

"And yet you have one less hole in you right now because of me."

I snap my fingers at him and motion for him to turn around. He does and I zip Dante's arms behind him.

Together, we walk into the bar. Riley already has another beer, and Stalin enters from outside holding a chunk of ice from the storm. He wraps it in a bar towel and holds it to his cheek.

"Stalin, man, I'm—"

Dante's words meet Stalin's wagging finger.

"Look, I'm sorry, but you just don't know..."

"Oh, what don't I know?" Stalin grabs Dante by the tattered sweatshirt. "I don't know how hard life is? You know who you're talking to, don't you? Or has working with the only openly gay man in a hundred-mile radius been hard on you, too?"

"Well, it—"

"Shut. Up. Dante."

For a second, I think Stalin is about put Dante's head in the last blade of the ceiling fan rotating right above them.

"You don't get to play martyr by proxy with me. I know your family, Dante. I know they've taken you back time and time again, no matter how dumb you act. Well, my family is either in the ground or wishing *I* was."

The air in the room goes from tingly to cold. Even the outside wind seems to diminish. A small tear forms in the corner of Stalin's right eye before flowing down his cheek and disappearing into his beard.

I want to say something. Anything. I want to tell him things get better. But Stalin's journey, like mine, is far from over. We both have more obstacles, roadblocks, and enemies to face. And (hopefully) even new friends.

I am not one to judge my fellow journeyman.

Riley puts his arm around Stalin and gives his neck a little squeeze. "Hey, I love ya, Battleship."

"Damn you, Cooter." Stalin wipes his eye and laughs. "Well, I love you like a sister because I only like men who have all of their teeth."

Riley smiles. "Technically, all of my teeth are in this bar."

Stalin chuckles, a low, little thing, but it's genuine.

"Okay, the roads are slicker'n shit. The whole state is in lockdown." The sheriff brushes past me and pushes Dante into a chair. "I can't take you anywhere tonight."

"Sheriff, can't we just let this go?" asks Dante, his voice quivering. "I mean, I didn't even have a loaded gun."

The sheriff shakes his head.

"I've got priors," Dante whines, "and I'm real sorry. If I could take it back, I would."

"Well, now." A smile crosses the sheriff's face that drops my stomach to my knees. "If you like, we can take care of this the other way."

Chapter Fifty-One

Trooper

NOW

I don't take the time to assess whether it's old blood from Riley's wounds or new blood from something else. I take off the brake, pump the clutch, and put it in first gear. The transmission groans at me as I shift too late. I haven't driven stick since I was thirteen, but that won't stop me now.

"Wait! Don't leave!" Riley's face in the glass is more panicked than mad, his eyes wide.

Maybe I should listen to him.

Then he shatters the side window with the butt of the ax.

I take the last chance of a civil conversation off the table by punching Riley in the face.

He falls back, and I press on the gas. Thankfully, this relic is rear wheel drive, so I lurch forward out of the garage.

"Don't leave me you—you bitch!"

Ever the romantic...

I pop the clutch and shift into 2nd, avoiding two downed trees on the right of the road but spinning out on the icy road in doing so. I try to correct it, but the car angles toward a ditch on the left.

"Mr. Bug, please don't do this..."

As I careen toward certain doom, the tires catch, and I swing the vehicle back onto the road.

I want to wipe my brow, but I need both hands on this rotted leather wheel.

I have almost no visibility. It's not just the sleet, but also the headlights. Either they are about to go out, or the battery is.

I just need to get to the bar to get help.

Not a mile out from the cabin, something on the side of the road catches my attention. I tap the brakes, so that I won't skid out on the ice.

It's a truck. A truck covered in branches and tree debris, as if someone was trying to hide it.

I put Mr. Bug in park and exit the vehicle. The sleet on my face cools me more than it bothers me. As I remove the limb on the front, it reveals a State of Mississippi Highway Patrol Tag.

This was the trooper's vehicle. But why is it covered up?

I remove other limbs and check the driver's side door. Locked. After slipping twice on the ice, I check the passenger door and find it unlocked. I almost slide in, then notice the seats.

In the night light, I see splotches of black covering them.

Shit. Did Riley kill the trooper? Is that the body I saw in the shed?

I shake my head and check for keys. I love you, Mr. Bug, but this vehicle is more end-of-the-world terrain ready. From floor to ceiling, I look and find jack shit. Now my fingerprints are all over this vehicle.

Stupid, stupid move, Rook.

I can't worry about that now. I hop back in Mr. Bug and gun it to the bar.

In the rearview window, I could swear I see a headlight in the distance.

Part Three:
Blizzard

The National Weather Service defines a blizzard as weather conditions that include sustained wind or frequent gusts up to 35 miles per hour or greater and/or has considerable falling/ blowing snow that reduces visibility. Seek shelter in a safe dwelling.

Caution Level: Extreme

Chapter Fifty-Two

Take a Knee

THEN

The words *'the other way'* send a chill up my spine icier than this winter storm.

"Boys, that work for you?" asks the sheriff.

Both Riley and Stalin open a fresh beer, take a swig, and sigh.

What the hell is going on?

"As much as I abhor violence, I still need a good janitor and a decent bartender, I guess." Stalin drains the entire can in three gulps. "If that's what he wants, I'll abide."

"Riley?"

"Let me stretch first, but, yeah." Riley pops his knuckles before putting one arm behind his head and pushing his elbow down with the other. Then he switches arms.

"Okay, what is happening?" I ask.

The sheriff purses his lips. "There's a Mississippi Code of Law from right around when it became a state. Maybe 1825 or '26 or so. It says that when a party is wronged, the group may seek restitution outside of a court if the guilty party agrees to such demands and refuses to press charges."

Oh, God, what is about to happen?

"Oh, I know that code." Dante shifts in his seat as if he is sitting on a dozen needles and swallows a lump in his throat. "What do you propose?"

"One lick." The sheriff's two words linger in the air.

"Oh, that's cool. Yeah, I hit Stalin with my gun, so he can—"

"For each of us."

And there it is. The sheriff's demon will get its blood today after all.

"This is barbaric," I say.

"It's better than sending Mr. Dante to jail." The sheriff pops his knuckles. "This will be his second strike?"

"Third," Dante mutters, hanging his head.

The sheriff lets out a whistle. "That's years, not days of time in Parchman."

"What's that?" I ask.

"A prison worse than death," Riley chimes in helpfully.

"Can't we just let this slide?" I ask. "Look, he didn't even shoot anyone."

"City of Columbus has a steeper fine for waving a gun in public than firing one," the sheriff offers.

"I just can't—"

Dante's sunburnt head taps my side interrupting me like a dog trying to snuggle in as an apology. "It's okay." Dantes mumbles.

"It's really not."

"Look, this is just Southern justice."

I look around for something—anything—from the men around me. Stalin looks sad, his shoulders drooped. Riley hops from foot to foot, a boxer about to enter the ring.

Only the sheriff stands stoic, his arms crossed and flat eyes on me.
As my stomach turns. "Okay."
Then the sheriff pulls Dante out of the chair.
"Just take a knee, and this will all be over soon."

Chapter Fifty-Three

The Box

NOW

Mr. Bug's heater is no joke. I go from freezing to sweltering in the time it takes me to get to Stalin's Bar. I keep checking my rearview mirror for any other cars, but I guess I imagined the headlights behind me.

At the bar, the sheriff's truck is still there. At this point, I don't care if he arrests me. I need help. I put Mr. Bug into park and hop out, trying to figure out what the hell I'm going to tell them.

Sit-Rep: I have at least two, maybe three different people's blood on me. I have a warrant out for my arrest. The less I say, the better off I am.

I leave Mr. Bug's engine running because I honestly don't know if he will crank again. If things go south—well, further south—I still need an escape route.

Maybe there's a jacket or something I can put on over my clothes, so I don't look like I just survived *The Texas Chainsaw Massacre*. There's nothing in the car but 8-track tapes of the *Oak Ridge Boys* and *The Lawrence Welk Show*. I pop the trunk.

And that's when I see it. In the center of the spare tire that has cables running from it for some strange reason, is a mahogany box about the size of a shoebox.

It has a single brass clasp holding it shut.

I open it.

Inside are tiny jars like you see jams and jellies in at a restaurant. Single-serving stuff. All I see are the lids and dates written on them.

I've never known someone who had to have road jellies but to each their own...

I take one out to examine it and immediately wish I hadn't.

The box drops from my shaking hand into the trunk, splaying its contents and secrets around the spare tire.

The jar in my hand has fallen out too, but into the ice, flipping end-over-end until it smashes into the icy concrete. I'm unfazed by the crashing glass, and even the *sploosh* of liquid on my leg.

It's the emerald-colored eye that rolls out and lands on my shoe that has me shitting my pants.

Chapter Fifty-Four

The Basket

NOW

Nothing makes sense anymore.

Of course, it's not like anything that happened tonight was *normal,* but this is beyond the pale.

I gasp, just now realizing I haven't taken a breath since I saw the green eye.

The eye has locked on me. Without a lid, it is as wide as an eye can get. It just looks shocked, maybe even accusatory. What do I do? Do I pick it up? It's clearly evidence, however I'm the one driving a stolen car...

Without thinking further, I kick the eye off into the distance and close the trunk. The top thing is getting the lady and Riley the help-slash-incarceration they both desperately need.

But how do you tell a sheriff that you just dropped a bookcase on a serial killer? I doubt they make Hallmark greeting cards for that.

I gather what wits I can and enter the bar.

The sheriff is checking his radio and Stalin is filling up empty buckets with sink water. I guess the weather has thawed the pipes for the water to run now. And the old lab Cotton is still in the back of the room, sound asleep on his bed.

"Hey, welcome back. Want some more tequila?" Stalin says casually before getting a good look at me. At the sight of me, he dashes my way. "What the hell happened?"

"I've been worse," I lie. Since they last saw me, I've earned a few more bruises, gashes, and stab wounds, I guess. "Sheriff, I need you to call in the police."

"Not a problem, Ms. Craddock." The sheriff leaves his barstool and strolls my way. "And maybe you can give me back those IDs you took from my pocket."

"Ah, well, screw it, sure." I reach into my pants and fling them at him like I'm dealing him two poker cards. "You know what? Fine, take it. I don't care. I don't care anymore! Look, dammit, Riley has some lady captive at her house. He's probably killed a state trooper, and she tried to kill me, so..."

"Shh..." Stalin gives me a bear hug. Normally, I'd push someone away for trying to calm me down, but his wrapping his giant arms around me and giving me the gentlest of squeezes makes me want to cry. "Sheriff, can you radio this in?" he asks.

"Ten-four." The sheriff opens the door and stops in his tracks, letting cold gusts enter the bar, flickering some candles that are keeping the place lit. I only can catch a glimpse of the sheriff in the mirror at the end of the bar, but something has him shaken.

He shuts the door and turns to face us.

"Where did you get the car, Rook?"

It takes me a second to realize he didn't call me *Ms. Craddock* for once.

"From the cabin—I mean the garage—of the lady," I admit, pushing back softly from Stalin and meeting the sheriff's furrowed brow.

"She tried to stab me, well, she actually did stab me, but I had a bottle of de-icer in my shirt that took most of the damage."

The sheriff makes his way closer. "So, you stole a car?"

"Well, yes, but she stabbed me, and I was only able to get away because I dropped a bookshelf on her..."

The impact of the sheriff's backhand on my face knocks me to the ground. Stalin steps forward. "Sheriff, now..."

The sheriff attempts to brush past Stalin, but Stalin holds him back. The sheriff plants a kick into Stalin's left knee, knocking the giant to the ground. Even wounded, Stalin grabs the sheriff's belt and holds him from what he's been reaching for.

The basket with the sheriff's revolver.

I crawl up from the floor and run to the bar's front door. The moment I grab the knob, the door swings open. I stumble back as someone enters from the other side.

"You've got to be shitting me."

The line is a cliché, but hell if I can think of something more clever with Riley's nine-millimeter aimed at my face.

Chapter Fifty-Five

Shitkicker

THEN

The storm outside slams branches against the tin roof. It sounds like fingernails on a chalkboard.

"Can't I get a minute?" asks Dante, the realization of what is about to happen apparently hitting him. "Or can I get a shot or something?"

"Nope." The sheriff pushes down on Dante's shoulder. "Pain is one hell of a teacher, so it's best we be on with the lesson."

The man drops to his right knee and looks up.

"Ladies first."

I hadn't even noticed I was pacing. I grab a bottle of Goldschläger off the shelf, tear off the top, and down two big gulps of cinnamon liquor. Then I give a swig to Dante.

The sheriff glares at me, but I will not make this worse than it already is.

I step up to Dante. A few tears are already in his eyes. I ball up my fist and tap his chin so slowly even I barely feel it.

"There."

"That's not gonna cut it, little lady."

"Sorry, I hit like a girl." I step back and spread my arms wide. "Plus, I set him on fire, so consider us square."

The sheriff chuckles. "Of course, that same Mississippi Code only gave the right to men, not women, but I'm all about equality and that other liberal shit."

I grab the bottle of Goldschläger and down two more big gulps. "Well, bless your bleeding heart, sheriff."

The next up is Stalin. His glazed-over eyes say those last three beers were steeling him for this. The big man walks over to Dante, who closes his eyes. Stalin balls up his fist, pulls his shoulder back, and swings.

The sound like two ribeye steaks slapping fills the room. It's not an over-the-top punch. With Stalin's stature and upper body strength, he could've taken out some teeth. This punch is more about an eye-for-an-eye. Or, in Stalin's case, a punch to the jaw for a shotgun butt to the face.

Instead of backing away, Stalin waits for Dante's gaze to meet his. Both men nod, and Stalin grabs his beer.

"Cooter," the sheriff calls like a coach calling a kid off the bench to play.

Riley finishes his beer and crushes the can against his skull. He strolls over to Dante and, without stopping his momentum, lands a right punch across Dante's face.

The sound of bone popping makes my eyes squeeze tight. But Dante isn't the one screaming.

"Shit! Ow! Shit! Shit! Shit-shit!" Riley holds his hand. Even from across the room, I can see one of his knuckles indented. Stalin walks over to him and grabs his hand.

"Oh, that's tough, Cooter." Riley squirms as Stalin digs his thumbs into Riley's hand and glances over Riley's shoulder. "Say, it looks like a nice lady is coming in from the storm."

"Where?" When Riley turns his head, Stalin jams his thumbs into Riley's hand and a pop like a bottle rocket going off brings out curses from everyone.

"Ah! You asshole!" Riley pushes away from Stalin and shakes the fire out of his hand. "You could've warned me!"

"Then you would've screwed it up." Stalin hands Riley an unopened beer, and Riley places the cold can on his hurt hand. "Also, I don't take insurance, so this is gonna cost you out of pocket."

"Eat me."

The sheriff strolls over to his captive. The sheriff's hat blocks out the overhead light, casting Dante in shadow. With one hand, the sheriff raises Dante's jaw. Then he balls up his left fist and lands a punch dead center, crushing Dante's nose.

Blood and spit fly, covering Riley and me in a spray of crimson.

Dante screams. "You bwoke my nose!"

"Some debts require blood," the sheriff says simply, cutting the zip tie binding Dante.

The sheriff's radio squawks, and he walks outside. As Dante stumbles up to the bar, Riley pops open a beer and hands it to him. I pass Dante a dish towel with ice in it, and Stalin slides over a bottle of Ibuprofen.

Dante nods at each of us.

The wind beating against the window increases. I'd almost forgotten about the storm. Beating a man will do that, I guess.

After a long pull on his beer, Dante asks, "You want me to fix that window?"

Stalin leans across the bar and puts his head in his hands. "So, you're just gonna rob me and then go back to work like nothing happened?"

"The worst you can say is *no*, right?"

Stalin pushes back and stares at the tin roof. "Just go home."

"You got it, boss."

As I take another swig of Goldschläger, it occurs to me how drunk I've gotten in the last five minutes. Maybe it's the adrenaline leaving my body. Or maybe it is that I'm drinking the alcohol equivalent of the candy Red Hots like they're going to turn into a pumpkin at midnight.

I try to slide the open bottle of Goldschläger down the bar, but it catches on something and tips.

"Shit!" I dart over to set it upright, stopping the liquid from glugging out of the bottle and all over the ground. "I'm pretty drunk."

"I got so drunk once I banged a papaya," Riley chimes in.

"Is that some racial slang or something?" I ask, not quite sure I heard that right.

"Nope." He swigs his beer and sighs. "But it *is* why they won't let me back in the Piggly Wiggly."

I've only known the guy for, what, two, three hours? And, somehow, this doesn't shock me.

"I thought you banged that horse," Stalin adds, "and that's why you can't go to the rodeo."

"Nope. That was Stevie. And he only killed that horse. The paper printed that someone had killed, and then sodomized the horse. Stevie came forward, not to turn himself in, but to set the record straight. He was later quoted in the paper saying *I didn't rape no horse.*"

"How commendable," I say. "Did the paper ever print a retraction?"

"Oh, yeah, but he still sued them for defamation of character." Riley takes a pull from his beer. "Stevie was oddly surprised he lost that case."

"And yet he killed a horse." I hang my head.

"Yep." Stalin's voice is low, yet accepting, like someone let air out of his lungs without him knowing.

Riley raises his beer and I, too drunk to care, raise the vodka bottle. He says, "Only in the Delta."

Stalin and I respond, "Only in the Delta."

After a gulp, the sheriff reenters. "Okay, gang, get to where you're going. The storm has a thirty-minute window and the ground's temp hasn't dropped too much."

"Since I live here, I'm staying." Stalin points around the bar. "Got heat, power, and the walls are up. Anybody else? Rook?"

"I'd rather be anyone than here, Battleship." My words slur as I eye the Goldschläger and consider another swig.

The sheriff checks his watch. "I'll hang here until I go make my rounds. Told dispatch I would wait a bit in case they need me to pull some dumbass out of a ditch or something."

"I've got a cabin I'm staying at nearby." Riley smiles at me and a little blood trickles out from his lost tooth. "You want to come? Got a guest room and everything."

I am just sober enough to remember I have Riley's keys.

But, the alcohol whispers dangerously, *maybe he's not as bad as I initially thought.*

If Riley tries to leave, he'll look for his keys. However, if I *find* them, maybe I can drive us.

"Sure." I take two steps toward him and stumble, all the Gold-schläger hitting me at once.

The sheriff catches me by the arm.

"My passenger seat's seatbelt is loose," Riley says.

"Oh, who needs 'em?" I ask.

An arm under mine lifts me. The sheriff surprises me and then says, "I'll help you out to the Shitkicker."

"The Shitkicker?" I ask, my words slurring into a casserole of mumbles.

"Riley has...well...you'll see."

"Hold up." Riley takes out his pill bottle, crushes one on the counter under a beer bottle, and snorts it.

Sit-Rep: I am too drunk to care.

As the sheriff walks me out into the cold, the sleeting rain pelts my face. My foot slips on the icy ground, but the sheriff catches me. Unfortunately, it is by the back of my bra strap. Now my boobs feel strangled and I have a rugburn under my armpits from the sports bra.

Riley opens the door to the Shitkicker: a Suzuki Sidekick. It looks like a matchbox car and a Lego had a baby. As I plop down in the front passenger seat, the entire thing rocks.

Is this thing made of plastic?

The sheriff tries to buckle me in. I swat his hand away too late to motion that I can do this shit myself. However, we are both confused by the over-the-chest seatbelt.

"Damnation, Riley, how's this thing lock?" asks the sheriff.

Riley replies, "Um, it don't."

The sheriff takes out his handcuffs. He cuffs the belt together, then tosses the key to Riley.

Why the hell wouldn't he have given me the keys?

Finally, the sheriff takes my hand in his and gives me a pat. "You be safe now, Ms. Craddock, you hear?"

I swear that is the most Andy Griffith Show *line you could've said.*

The sheriff shuts the door as I notice how iced over the windshield is. My mind flashes as I realize I have the keys to the vehicle. I crank the engine and cut on the defrost on full blast.

From outside the vehicle, Riley and the sheriff exchange words I can't hear. I can't tell if the sheriff is trying to be protective of me, or possessive. I just need to get out of here before he notices those playing cards in his pocket instead of my licenses.

When Riley does return to the vehicle, he puts my bass guitar in the back, and then sits down in the driver's seat. As he shuts the door and looks at me, he asks, "How did you crank the Shitkicker?"

"I turned the keys in the ignition."

Technically, that's not a lie.

His eyes study me. I want to break his stare, but I know that might show that I just had his keys the whole time. Then he smiles, and a trickle of blood drips down his cheek.

"I knew I'd just done something stupid like that!" He puts the car in Reverse without putting on his own seatbelt. "Next stop, home sweet home!"

I slump back in the vehicle, my shoulders relax, and I breathe deep.

As the darkness of sleep approaches, I *think at least the hard part of the night is over.*

Chapter Fifty-Six

Better Pray to God

NOW

"Whatever this whore's said, don't you dare trust her, Sheriff." Riley's eyes narrow in on me as his gunsight sways side to side. I doubt he's nervous. More likely, he's just done another bump of his *medicine* because his breathing is a series of rapid, quick breaths. The lone headlight of a four-wheeler illuminates him from behind.

"Come. Here."

Sit-Rep: Riley is whacked out of his brain and has me dead to rights. The sheriff either has his revolver or Stalin does, which means I can't exit the back way. There is a beer bottle one step to my right. Now if I can just—

A thunderous boom interrupts my plans.

I expect to see a trickle of smoke come from Riley's gun as I am about to find myself with one extra hole in my body. Not finding a new orifice, I wonder if the storm has possibly turned from sleet to something more violent.

That's when I hear the groan. I turn as Stalin holds his stomach. A growing crimson spreads across his blue overalls. He looks up in disbelief as he collapses face first onto the floor.

Before any of us can react, Cotton's teeth clamp down on Riley's shooting arm, eliciting a scream from him as he scrambles to rid himself of the dog. The sheriff retrieves his gun from the basket yet again, just as Riley hammers the butt of his gun into Cotton's head, sending the dog off with a whimper.

"Cooter, if you're done tying your own rope there..." The sheriff squares up and holsters his revolver. The slide of steel on leather dances through the room with a *whiffp* sound, one that is quiet, yet distinctive. The sheriff smiles while lowering his gaze to just below his Stetson. His eyes narrow as he rolls his shoulders back. "...I need to know if you believe in God."

Sweat drips down the left side of Riley's face as his panicked eyes dart between me and the sheriff. His gun trembles as if a passing train is shaking the bar.

"Riley, drop the gun." My words are more of a whispered prayer than a command. Riley rocks his head in response, and I can see the muscles in his forearm tense as he grips the gun tighter.

"Sheriff, you just stay calm, and everything will be alright."

"This is one of two important questions that I ask because, in five seconds, one of us is gonna meet our Maker. You've got an appointment that you're over a decade late for. That was on me. Now, if you're faster than I am, well, so be it. I'm not afraid to die. I'm good with the Lord. Whatever happens to me, happens. The second question, well, this one requires action over words. Do you want to lower your gun and draw, or do you want to just take a knee?"

Riley keeps his gaze on the sheriff but keeps his gun on me.

"It was always gonna go down like this, wasn't it?" Riley's question floats through the bar as the two men square off.

Then, the moment Riley jerks the barrel of his gun the sheriff's way, a flash like something out of a Western movie occurs. The movement is fluid, as if years of practice are being called for in this one second. The sheriff draws his revolver, kicks one leg back, bends his knees slightly, fires from the hip, and then holsters it again.

As the sheriff wipes his hands together, my gaze goes back to Riley.

Riley's head tilts my way. It looks just like the T1000 in *Terminator 2* when Arnold or Sarah shot the morphing robot pointblank with a shotgun in the face. A hole the size of a baseball is where his left eye and cheek were. Through the hole I can clearly read the outline of the bar's sign: *Damn, We Closed.*

"Run..."

The word followed by a gush of blood escapes Riley's mouth as it looks as if someone has removed his spine. He crumbles to the floor. The gun smacks against the wood floor and clatters to within grabbing distance. The moment my hand grabs it, a boot smashes down onto my wrist. Something pops and I scream. The sheriff yanks me up by my collar and slams my face down on the closest table. The *fwip* of a zip tie on my left wrist precedes the *fwip* of the other.

Even though I am facedown, I watch the sheriff go through Riley's pockets. He grabs the gold pocket watch from Riley's front pocket and chuckles.

"Knew it."

The sheriff spins me around and leans into my face. His eyes are as dark as night and as hot as hell itself.

"You're taking me to where you got that car, and you better pray to God that my mother is still alive."

Chapter Fifty-Seven

Another Mess

NOW

When you find yourself zip-tied in the backseat of a murderer's truck, you can't help but reflect on recent events. I play the night over and over in my head. What I perceived in both Riley and Stalin as *respect* for the sheriff was actually fear. When I stopped him from shooting Dante, the sheriff wasn't worried whether Dante was armed or not. He just wanted to kill someone.

Anyone. Shoot, he would have killed Dante, if I hadn't yanked the gun away.

How did I downplay this level of...evil?

And more to the point, how did I miss the relationship between the lady and the sheriff? It is as clear as day now, down to the movie posters in the kid's bedroom.

Coogan.

Blazing Saddles.

And, of course, *High Noon.*

Of course they were all Westerns, the same Westerns I'd watched with my gramma. She'd sit in her recliner wearing my grandfather's robe. The one that smelled like sandalwood and coffee, the scents of his daily rituals: aftershave and caffeination.

In these *particular* Westerns though, the hero was always the sheriff.

"Look, your mother tried to *kill* me," I plead from the backseat, trying and failing to find any give in the zip ties. "I think she's done this before—."

"Shut your whore mouth."

"She's crazy and—"

The back of a balled-up fist clocks my left cheek and eye so hard my head careens into the side glass.

The sheriff never takes his eyes off the road. "Never speak ill of my mother."

As the taste of rusty pennies fills my mouth, I spit blood on my passenger window. I would rather spit in the sheriff's eye, but I only want to insult him, not crash the truck.

A rage hits me. "Why don't you just kill me?"

"Oh, don't worry your little head." The vehicle swerves around a downed limb, not slowing in the slightest. "You're going to die tonight, Ms. Craddock. It's just a matter of how much suffering you've earned before the lights go out."

"Well, Riley was the one who had your mother locked up in her room like a hostage."

The sheriff keeps quiet.

"And he's no longer in the picture, so..."

The sheriff grinds his teeth and that's when it hits me.

"You did this."

The truck swerves around a downed tree. We continue forward.

"Mom, was, well, getting a little too stabby in her old age."

The sheriff laughs to himself about God knows what.

"And I got tired of cleaning up her messes." He hangs his head as he adds, "So damn tired..."

The plastic zip ties dig into my wrists as I turn and twist. If only I had something sharp to cut into them, maybe a sharp edge or saw, I could get free.

But what then?

As the driver's side windshield wiper catches, then snaps, the sheriff rolls down the window. The biting sleet hits his face, yet he never flinches as he yanks the blade off and tosses it into the woods.

"And you're just another mess I'm gonna have to scrape off my shoe."

Chapter Fifty-Eight

Gone

NOW

The outline of the single-story cabin approaches through the mist, the truck's headlights bouncing along the empty gravel road. Nothing but ice and woods fill my peripheral. Any hope I had that my interrupted 911 call might have brought someone—anyone—to the cabin, dies on the vine.

There are no new cars when we arrive at the cabin.

No one will save you but you.

As we approach the house, I try a last bit of reason.

"Look, right there, under that brush, is a state trooper's truck!" The sheriff keeps his eyes on the prize. "And I think his body is in the shed in the back, and I'm pretty sure Riley killed him!"

"No," the sheriff rubs his beard with one hand before he responds. "Riley only knocked the guy out."

"Well, great! Let's go get him and he can help us."

"That's...not an option anymore."

"I don't get it..." Then, I *do* get it. "You? You killed him?"

"The door to the shed was open, and he'd have frozen to death in this weather." The sheriff swerves around a downed limb, but then rights the vehicle before it skids. "Probably."

"Did you know I was in the house?" I ask.

"Didn't." The sheriff chuckles. "Would've made everything much easier if I had."

I ask the redundant question of, "That was you knocking on the interior wall?"

"Naw. Probably mama. Sometimes I just smack the cabin's interior walls because it echoes throughout all the walls. It's well built. Sometimes that's just easier than talking to mother."

"Why didn't you go inside and check on your mom?"

"Uh..." The noise from the sheriff is more of a growl than a grumble. "I thought she somehow got out and then attacked this trooper during a welfare check. Going inside, well, it'd be a whole thing...I wasn't in the headspace to deal with her bullshit."

"*Her bullshit*? You killed an unconscious, innocent man. You asshole..."

The sheriff raises his right fist. I flinch and he stops it an inch from my face. Even with a stopped up and bloody nose, the stale beer and heat escaping his pores assault my senses. The sheriff only takes his hand away when we arrive at the cabin, and he puts the truck in Park.

He exits his truck and heads to my side of the vehicle. I lock the door with my foot, but he has the keys, so he unlocks it and grabs my flailing legs. With one heave, I crash into the icy ground below.

He stands above me and flips open his jacket flashing his holstered revolver, a reminder of what he is capable of.

As he towers above me, he sucks his teeth and, sounding almost in pain he asks, "Are you going to continue to be difficult?"

"No." *I am, I just haven't decided how yet.*

The sheriff rolls me over so that my knees are under me. A pain stabs them— it's the ice, thick on the leaves below me, somehow oddly beautiful even as they jab me. The cracking of trees and branches in the distance reminds me that nowhere is safe tonight.

With a hand in my armpit and a heave, I'm on my feet. I slip on the ice, but the sheriff keeps his hand on my shoulder, pushing me forward toward the door, still slightly ajar from my prior escape.

"If she's hurt, you're hurt."

"Put it on my tab." Fake bravado won't save my ass but it's all I've got at the moment.

"What was that?"

"Nothing."

The lights are off in the cabin. Maybe the power went out again. The sheriff flicks the light switch. Nothing. He grabs a flashlight from his utility belt and clicks *On*.

"Ma?" The sheriff's voice cracks slightly. Concern and maybe a hint of...fear? Maybe it's for her being dead, but maybe it's also because she might be alive and pissed.

"About damn time," comes a grumble from under the bookcase.

The sheriff drops the flashlight and dashes to his mother. Taking a chance, I make for the front door.

I'm one foot out when the doorknob explodes from a bullet.

"Get over here."

I turn and stomp to the sheriff.

"Help me lift this."

"With what hands?"

"Just crouch and use your shoulder."

The sheriff puts his revolver on the ground, squats and puts both of his hands on the shelf. I crouch and hook my right shoulder under the bookshelf's edge.

Together, we lift.

Once the bookcase reaches the top of its ascent, the sheriff steps to the center, careful not to step on his mother. The revolver is within my grasp, but I can't do dick with it if I try to shoot from behind my back.

The same isn't true for the lady's WWII Buddha knife, which is also within grasp. I snatch it up as casually as I can, then shove its blade into my waistband behind my back and cover the hilt with my shirttail.

The sheriff finishes propping up the bookcase and glances at the revolver, then back at me.

"You thought about it, didn't you?"

I nod, and he picks up the gun, holstering it.

"First smart thing you've done all night, Ms. Craddock."

The sheriff tilts his head toward the sofa, and I take the hint and a seat. He is on all fours checking on his mama. In this instant, he's not a murderer. The lady on the floor is not a serial killer. For these two, the rest of the world has stopped. Right now, this is merely a boy helping his hurt mother.

Then, as if she's shot out of a cannon, this *hurt mother* is on my chest, strangling me into the couch.

"Why'd you do that, you green eye?"

Her breath hasn't improved in the last hour, but the rage in her eyes is more concentrated. She stares at me like I kicked her childhood dog, cut off her pigtail, and stole her boyfriend all in the same day.

My eyes catch the sheriff's. With crossed arms, he checks his watch.

"Ma, are you hurt?"

"I'm hurt, not injured, Junior." Her cold, bony hands are practically in my throat. Her fingertips are so far up that they feel like they are in my damn skull. And all of her ninety pounds are shutting off the oxygen to my brain. "I've just got to teach this one a lesson before I take what she doesn't deserve."

I twist my arms and grab my only hope. The knife in my hand won't cut fast enough. Darkness creeps into my vision, an unwelcome fog overtaking me. The burning in my chest from trapped, dead air yearning to escape, builds.

Then the knife slips from my grip and slides off the back of the couch. I hear it thump against the carpet.

So do the lady and the sheriff.

"What the hell was that?" The sheriff follows his question as he kneels down and glances under the couch.

The noise isn't enough to stop the lady's death grip, but it loosens it. With a trickle of bad air out and good air in, I spot Riley's ax. Correction, the state trooper's. It is two steps away. I know I get one shot at this. With the sheriff distracted, I slam my knee into my attacker's chest. All the air that I wish I had exits her chest and she crumples over.

I'm on my feet by the time the sheriff looks up from under the sofa. I plant my right leg in his skull so hard I would've made a fifty-yard field goal with that kick. The cop tumbles back spitting out blood and teeth.

I raise my foot to stomp on him, but that's when a little voice in my head tells me to turn and look. I lower my foot and am more upset by what I don't see than what I do.

The lady is gone.

Chapter Fifty-Nine

Run

Last Year

Seventeen minutes. Seventeen crucial, soul-crushing minutes. A period of just over a quarter of an hour that changed my life.

And I can't remember a single second of it.

I can't remember anything after Gramma clutched her chest. Everything after that was as if my brain was a kid's Etch A Sketch. Someone grabbed it and shook it with all the anger that would swell up inside me later.

The next thing I knew, I was the one in a hospital bed with blood all over my chest and arms. From what I was told by the firemen who broke through the adjacent wall to get to us, I sliced open both of my wrists trying to break free of the handcuffs. The cuts were so deep that a piece of the steel cuff on the right side hit the bone.

Besides my now bandaged hands and wrists, my left shoulder was dislocated and the brachialis muscle in my right elbow was torn.

Once a doctor checked me out and a nurse stitched me up, someone helped me to a hospital bed. It took me another nine minutes to realize where I was: the exact same chute that Gramma was in when we first got here.

Had we stayed in the chute, she would've had immediate medical attention after the heart attack. Gramma would've gotten an adrenaline shot or CPR or the damn paddles or something else lifesaving and none of this would've happened.

Had I not done what I did, Gramma would still be alive.

None of this was real. The strobing orange lights had to be just a bad trip. Clearly, someone had drugged me. All of this was an acid trip or LSD or roofies.

And that's when I saw it: in the chair to the left of my bed, was the one thing that would ground me. As high as I wanted to fly away in my imagination, this anchored me. Tore me from my hope and slapped me across the face with a brick.

Gramma's robe. The one she wore every time we watched a movie, a Western, together. The one she wore into the ER. And the one she would never wear again.

We must've left it when we moved from out of this chute. I was just so ecstatic that Gramma was going to get better treatment that I practically floated all the way to the private room.

The way the robe looked so soft, so welcoming, so safe, forced me back into my bed. An invisible elephant planted its giant ass on my chest and was crushing not just my lungs and heart, but my soul.

I screamed and attempted to shake the pain from my brain. However, my strapped-down arms only added to my torment.

There was an envelope next to the hat. Even though I couldn't reach it, the words Federal and a code of MCL 600.8511(e) were on it. It didn't take a genius to know that the sealed document had something to do with those agents and my falsifying Gramma's insurance.

Gramma.

Just the thought of what I did, and what—no, who—I lost, soured my stomach. I leaned as far over as a trapped person could and vomited onto a tray on the side table. Most of that funk made it into the tray, anyway. I sweated and salivated, but before I could dry heave again, my curtain opened, and Thomas entered.

"Thomas, one day, you're going to see me at my best," I said, wiping my mouth on my shoulder.

He angled his head outside of my tent of despair. After a quick glance around, he closed the curtain and rushed to my side.

"Okay, you're going to have, like, three minutes..." he said.

"Three minutes until what?" I wiped my eyes as he undid the strap on my right wrist.

"What's going on?" I asked, as he unlocked my left one.

Thomas pushed me upright and shoved my clothes in my arms.

"Get dressed." He reached into his wallet and yanked out all the cash he had. "Take this. I'd give you my credit card, but then they could link us, track your movements, and I could get in trouble."

"Please, slow down, and tell me what's going on!"

Thomas shoved his hand over my mouth and mouthed a shh at me.

"Look, I'm sorry about your Gramma."

Thomas turned me around and lifted the hospital gown off me as he slipped my Tupac t-shirt on me, the one with the words 2Pacalypse Now under the rapper's scowling mug.

"And I'm sorry I planted that stupid idea in your head that she needed better insurance. But you've got to get out of here. The storm killed one of those federal agents that came to arrest you in the crane accident. The other is in ICU. I heard that one talking with the duo that came to replace him. And they're coming to take you away."

I slipped on my panties, then jeans, and finally socks and shoes.

As he shoved the cash in my pocket, I locked with his ocean-colored eyes. In that second, I took a chance. I placed the biggest kiss on him. Yes, I'd thrown up in the last five minutes. And, yes, I hadn't brushed my teeth in a few days. It wasn't my best kiss. It also wasn't my worst.

Thomas held my hands in his hands, tears building in the corner of his eyes. He planted a kiss on my forehead and whispered the word that would become my mantra for the next year.

"Run."

So, I did just that. I ran. I got a fake ID from a creepy old guy in a leather jacket who worked as a bouncer at a dive bar outside of Toledo. He didn't want money, just a hand job. That was good for me because I doubt the thirteen dollars and eight cents I had to my name would've gotten me what I needed to disappear.

Chapter Sixty

The Devil Himself

NOW

It's no good. The lady's nowhere in the room.

I stick with my half-baked plan and dash over to the ax, grab it and hurry back into the lady's room. Using my shoulder, I shut the door behind me.

It won't slow the sheriff down more than a second or two, but that's something to work with.

Fumbling in the dark, I snake my hands down the handle until I reach the ax's head. My pinky finger grazes the edge of the blade and confirms how sharp it is. I put the blade against the plastic zip tie and step back from the wall.

Three...two...one...go!

As I slam the ax head into the wall, the zip tie cuts free. So does a layer of skin under my right forearm.

I stifle a scream at the huge chunk of skin sheered from my arm.

Shit-shit-shit!

The blood seems to seep through the skin rather than gushing. I dart over to the dresser and, grabbing an old T-shirt that reads *Crosstie* from it, take a pass at making a piss-poor tourniquet.

Something in the room shifts. Maybe it is the air, or the lights may have flickered. Just like lightning before thunder, I register the click of a gun's hammer snapping into place. Without thinking, I dive to the right. The wall in front of me, complete with the black wooden makeup dresser, explodes as a million holes pop out. Mirrors, powder, and glass bottles shatter as I hit the ground.

A trail of smoke creeps out from under the bed as my eyes meet those of the lady.

"I forgot I even owned this gun!" The giddiness in her voice floats through the room. "And I've got another batch of buckshot just for you, green eye!"

I mumble, "Does everyone in Mississippi own, like, forgotten guns?"

Not waiting around to find out, I make for the broken window to get the hell out of here.

A gloved hand wraps around my neck and another slams into my stomach, keeping me in the doomed room.

"It's rude to refuse a present." Blood covers the sheriff's beard. "Ma, where do you want her?"

"Well, hold on, I'm kind of stuck under the bed."

I reach for the sheriff's holstered revolver, but he swats my hand away and tosses me on the ground. With a thump, the sheriff grabs his mother by the arms and pulls her, and the double-barreled shotgun, out from under the bed.

Sit-Rep: I have two armed killers in one room with two possible exits. The window is closer, and the hallway is too narrow to avoid gunfire. The lady has one round of buckshot left in that double-barrel. If the sheriff hasn't reloaded his gun since earlier tonight, he has three hollow point rounds left. The ax is my only hope, but that's only if I have one, not two, heavily armed problems.

From the remains of the makeup vanity, I spot my chance.

As the lady cocks the hammer, I snatch a handful of glass and foundation powder the consistency of dust. Then I fling everything in the faces of my attackers.

A cloud of glass and powder assaults the sheriff, and he reaches for his revolver. His mother just fires blindly. Most of the blast shoots past me, destroying everything in its path.

But two pieces of buckshot make it to my left shoulder, followed by searing pain. It is like getting hit by a tiny bull made of searing, angry fire. First comes the impact, taking balance, breath, and equilibrium with it as I crash into the ground. Next comes the burning of the hot rounds destroying nerve clusters in my upper body. A thousand hot pokers spread through my shoulder as nausea builds in me because I JUST GOT SHOT!

I scream and my left hand involuntarily shakes, possessed by the demon Winchester or whoever made the unwelcomed lead in my body. There's blood on the carpet, which means there's a good chance the bullets went straight through my body. I don't know much, but in movies that's a good sign.

I put pressure on the entry wound with one hand. My back will just have to bleed for now. With the other hand, I barely grab the ax because my arm is numb. I take a chance on the hallway exit.

A revolver round blasts the unlit hall light in the ceiling, showering me in glass shards.

The sheriff claws at his eyes, even though he holds the revolver in his hand. His mother crouches and dashes my way, a hellhound spider monkey coming after me like she's straight out of *The Shining*.

"She's mine."

"No, mama, I can make the shot."

"No, you won't," she yells, "You're mine!"

I scream as the lady jumps toward me, sending me stumbling backward down the hall. My back on the ground, I put everything into a double-footed kick sending her flying into her son. They both crash to the ground. As they do, the thunder roars.

I grab the ax head and use it as a cane to stand. The back of the lady's nightgown slowly morphs from off-white to pink. Then a darker red, a crimson-wine stain that engulfs her entire back.

"Mama?" The sheriff's voice is small, almost childlike, as he gets to his elbows, the smoke still puffing from the end of his gun. The sheriff's wide eyes lock with his mother's.

She takes a bloody hand and touches his cheek.

"Son..." She belts out a raspy, thick cough, spraying blood on his face. "Finish...her."

With that, her head collapses on the sheriff's chest.

The sheriff lets out a howl that gets into my soul. It's primal, one with a guttural pain. He hyperventilates until our eyes meet.

And I run like the devil himself is on my heels.

Chapter Sixty-One

Smartest Dumb Idea

NOW

Screaming, the sheriff fires what I hope is his last loaded round. The blast splits the handle of the ax, knocking it from my hand.

The sound of the revolver dry-clicking means this is my best chance. I grab the ax head and sprint into the living room, grabbing Riley's camo B.O.B. midstride to the cabin's back door.

A searing pain hits the back of my head, and I drop the ax as the sheriff's gun falls to the ground.

Even though he chucked it from across the room, the bear of a man is on me before I can even consider picking it up. With a bloodstain on the left side of his face, the rage in his white eyes pulses in the dimly lit room. Through gritted teeth, he spits and chokes me.

"You...bitch...".

Stars creeping into my vision, I kick the sheriff in the moneymaker with all the force I can muster, and he drops me.

I raise the half-ax above his head, but as I chop down the sheriff shifts, and the blade connects with the carpet. He drives a punch into my jaw. Something pops as blood fills my mouth and the taste of copper forces me to cough. I drop to my knees, in perfect eyeline with the sheriff.

I'm beyond exhausted.

He's running on pure hate.

As the sheriff rears back to punch me again, I hold up Riley's B.O.B. to block it. The bag absorbs the hit, and the last remaining contents from this bottomless bag fall onto the ground.

And that's when I see the ingredients to the smartest dumb idea I have in my arsenal.

Chapter Sixty-Two

Kneel

NOW

I grab what I can as I sprint toward the door. The sheriff catches my left foot, but I kick free.

Outside, I count my steps as I run into the darkness.

Once I get to the general area of my plan, I'm hoping to God that my count is accurate.

I turn back to face my attacker. To him, it looks like I'm just holding a silver bag against my chest and using the QuikClot on my shoulder wounds.

"There's so much more blood where that came from." In the doorway, the sheriff rips off his shirt and stands bare-chested. Hairy, hunched over, and filled with fury, his black-and-silver chest hair makes him appear more animal than man. The hot air leaving his lips looks like dragon fire in the cold.

I step into the silver blanket and zip it up as much as I can.

The sheriff lets out a deep and menacing laugh. "I'll kill you long before the cold does."

Under the light of a slit moon, I spot the knife in his hand. If he comes at me with it, my plan is for shit.

"I've got a question for you, Sheriff."

"Shoot." He rubs the blade against his chest, smearing blood across it.

"What color were your wife's eyes?"

Even from this distance, I can see a trickle of blood drip down his lip.

"Shut your whore mouth," he says, putting the knife into his belt loop. "A knife is too good for you."

He stomps my way. That's not good enough. He's mad.

I need rage, so I add kerosene to the fire that is the Sheriff.

"Were they the same color as your daughter's?"

Something snaps. The Sheriff lowers his head, his eyes beaming. No longer do I face a man. With his head tucked, I face a charging bull. I face a roaring bear.

Come on...come on...

I face something primitive. Something wholly powerful.

As he closes in, I do the one thing that will keep him angry, but give him a small victory. Something to keep him from thinking about anything else.

I kneel.

Chapter Sixty-Three

Icy Death

NOW

This act of submission cuts the fuel line to the sheriff's engine. He slows his run, then kicks his head back, laughs, and slow-claps.

"Now you're getting it." He extends his arms wide as sleet pelts his bare skin. "There's nowhere to run. No one can save you."

I lower my head, keeping one eye on him. I need him closer.

The sheriff breaks off an icicle hanging from a nearby branch. He chomps into it and points the sharp point my way. "And you, well, you're no killer, even though you did...you did kill..."

The brief reprieve of sanity is gone. His eyes narrow as he stomps toward me.

His footfalls go from heavy crunches near the entrance to the cabin to light pops and my prayers that he doesn't notice are answered.

When he finally stands in front of me, I laugh. It's not intentional. It's more like how a death row inmate flips everyone off right before the lever is thrown.

"What's so funny?"

The sheriff wraps both hands around my neck. The rough skin on his leathery hand is crushing sandpaper on my windpipe. I glance down. I need his feet to move just a bit closer to me.

"I was just thinking...two things..." I say through gasps of air. "One, how surprised...your mama was...when you killed her."

The sheriff lifts me, his arms pumping me in the air, stepping where I need him to.

At least I hope I'm right.

"Shut your whore mouth."

"It's...okay..." From where he holds me, the ice cracking underneath us is rhythmic, almost spiritual. I smile because for the first time since I arrived in this county, I am in control.

"And what's the second thing?"

"I'm remembering the...first compliment you...gave me...tonight ..."

He pulls me close, yet the sheriff still hasn't noticed my hands in the space blanket.

"And what was that?"

All the rage of the evening hits me. I've been stabbed, shot, throttled, and held captive, escaping one death trap after another. And now every fiber of my being focuses into one movement. I pull out the red ax head from the bag.

"This little thing has spunk."

Seeing it, the sheriff instinctively drops me.

I land on my knees, looking up at him with a smile.

Before he can act, I raise the ax head and slam it into the ice-covered pond under our feet, sending us both to an icy death.

Chapter Sixty-Four

The Last Thing

NOW

The pond shatters below our feet. I drop the ax head back into my space bag and, in the same move, pull the bag over my head. By the time the sheriff screams, the icy water drowns it out.

In the darkness of the space blanket, I feel a trickle of cold. There's a tear in the bag somewhere. I just have to hope the sheriff goes into hypothermic shock before I do.

Outside of the bag, the sheriff struggles in the water. His hands grab at the bag as his feet kick. I hold tight to the sides. This water is cold enough to kill.

At least that's what I'm counting on.

The sheriff's hands find my throat through the bag, though his grip is not nearly as tight as before. The cold water hits my legs, and an icy burn runs up between them.

The sheriff's grip lessens. Then it stops.

I take three quick breaths before opening the bag. The coldest water I've ever experienced pours in as I exit the bag. With one hand, I swim up. The other holds the bag.

In the cold darkness, there is something welcoming. Something forgiving.

It would be so easy to let go of everything right now.

Then, as I am about to accept my fate, there's something in the smell of the bag that lights a fire in me. It's a mixture of plastic and metal, like a hospital tray food tray. One that holds a weird meaning.

That's when I remember the last thing my grandmother said to me.

Chapter Sixty-Five

Fight Like You Are Wrestling the Devil Himself

LAST YEAR

The brain is a funny thing. I once read that this three-pound orb of jelly has something like 100 billion neurons. These nerve cells regenerate at an inch a month. Healing that protects our body from traumas, both physical and mental.

And that's why, sometimes, all it takes is one overpowering force, a sound, or even a smell or touch, to bring all that unfiltered shit back.

I remember Gramma grabbing her chest. I screamed and reached as far as my handcuffed hands would let me. For some reason, my face was an inch away from Gramma's recently eaten cafeteria food. I could smell the hot metal covers on the plastic tray. As for reaching Gramma, all I could connect with was her right big toe.

As her eyes clinched so hard that I thought her head would explode, she stopped. The ringing in my ears subsided as she dropped her hand from her chest. Gramma tilted her shaved head as her tired, kind, green eyes met mine. From her seated position on the back of the bed, she reached her hand toward mine. Even handcuffed, I tried to reach her fingers. Two different forces kept us apart, but we had to try.

As Gramma lowered her hand, she blinked and smiled. "I've got to go, Lil Hoody."

Never have so few words destroyed me so quickly. My body, from my pinky toe to the hair on head, quivered.

"O h - n o - n o - n o - G o d - n o - G r a m - ma-no-you're-fine-you're-fine-you're-fine..."

The words circled my mouth in a loop.

"Shh..."

Tears streaked down my face, and I shook the bad thoughts away. The same tears looked back at me from a face just like mine, only older. Wiser. And leaving.

"The-staff-they're-coming-they're-coming-they're-coming..." The words were a locomotive in my throat, rolling faster and faster than I could handle.

"Girl, don't try to hold back those tears. I've been in your seat. It's like holding a tissue over a crack in a dam. It's gonna come, and there ain't nothing wrong with crying. Anyone says otherwise can deal with me."

A rumble in my chest, my vehicle engine, roared. A mountain-leveling scream was building in not just my body, but my soul. Gramma must've sensed it because she hummed. I knew the tune from the first note: Swing Low, Sweet Chariot.

"Please..." The word was a hook cast into a vast ocean. A Hail Mary. A final plea.

"I can't stop this, Lil Hoody," Gramma says, her breath short yet determined. "And, honestly, I wouldn't if I could. I also can't stop the pain you're gonna go through. It will come. And it might be bad. Smothering. Overwhelming. But here's what I know: you are strong enough to get through it. Because I know you. Because I love you."

And then I leaned my head over Gramma's foot and wept. It wasn't a long weep, but it was one from my soul.

"You've always been a fighter, but this ain't a fight you need to worry about. I'm not scared." Gramma said as my nose touched her cold foot.

"Gramma, please, please..."

Gramma interrupted me as her eyes followed something across the ceiling. Something I couldn't see but, to Gramma, it was as real as I was.

"You remember why I call you Lil Hoody?"

I nodded, but then I asked for the story. One more time.

"When your parents died in that fire, well, there was this fireman. Fireman Rhett Van Namen. Fine strapping man. Good hair. No Belafonte, but you get me. Anyway, before he went in, I told him you were just a little thing. You were fourteen, no, thirteen months old. And he pulled you out of that fire. Wait. No. I said it wrong. He gathered you from that fire."

I leaned up from Gramma's foot and met her gaze. "He said that something in his gut, maybe intuition, maybe our good Jesus, who knows, told him to look in the kitchen. And that's where he found you. You had crawled into your parents' minifridge. A minifridge! Somehow, you closed it before the flames and smoke got too deep. You had just enough air in there to wait until this man, this stranger, did his duty and found you. When that fireman handed you to me, even though you already had a name from the moment you entered this world, you were my little Harry Houdini."

Despite the handcuffs, I tried to lean closer, to will my body to lie next to my Gramma.

Just one more time.

"You know, Houdini trusted his mind more than his body. My brain is the key that sets me free, he said. You did more than survive the blast; you saved yourself. You are your own key. And what a glorious key you are."

Even though my entire body felt like it was drowning and on fire at the same time, I said to Gramma, "Everything's going to be okay."

"Oh, I know it. And I'm kinda excited." She squeezed her hands together and looked at me with eyes I'd seen a million times, yet they shone brighter than ever before. "I love you, Lil Hoody. And I'll see you when you join me. But this isn't your fight. It's mine. And I'm done. I'm so tired, and now it's time for my reward. But you, you've got a long life ahead of you. I know it. Deep down, you will know when to fight, honey baby. Don't waste your energy on things that ain't worth a sliver of a thought. But, when the time comes, you use that energy. You fight. You fight like you are wrestling the devil himself."

And then, as if someone syphoned the light right out of her body, Gramma slumped over. Her body didn't collapse; it deflated. She left for home.

And, for the first time in my life, I was truly alone.

Chapter Sixty-Six

The Lock

NOW

I burst through the hole, spit water, and drag my ass and the bag up onto the ice. Literal icicles are forming in my breath. Uncontrollable shakes overtake me, but I turn to get my bearings.

That's when a fire shoots up my right calf. I scream and turn.

With the flaming devil's eyes locked on me, the sheriff's grin is almost as alarming as the Buddha knife buried in my leg.

I reach into the space bag as he yanks it out and raises it again.

That's when I bury the ax head into the center of his skull. As blood trickles down, a look of confusion crosses his face.

"Just take a knee," I say, grabbing the sheriff's shoulders, "and it will all be over soon."

With a half-smile, the man's eyes roll back into his head as he sinks under the water.

All the energy leaves my body. I collapse on the ice. The cabin might as well be a thousand miles away.

My heartbeat slows, and I look around at all of the beautiful sights this storm has brought.

I study the once-majestic trees, their limbs now bent like wet spaghetti. The powerlines sag, bass guitar strings loosened from their pegs. The grayish white of snow and ice of this beautiful destruction sends a sense of calm through my body.

And then I see it. It's about half the distance from where I am.

I stand, but my leg collapses. I don't know what the sheriff cut, but I'm losing blood fast. As I crawl to the storm shelter, I glance back at the trail of blood I'm leaving.

Maybe this will help someone find me, I think in a darkly optimistic way.

I'm losing feeling in my hands and arms, which don't perceive the ice all around. Each jerk of my body gets me closer to the shelter, but my strides are shortening. I'm losing steam, as well as blood.

My legs go numb, yet I keep moving.

And then, somehow, I'm in front of the storm shelter.

But that little bit of joy leaves me as I can't get the lock to turn.

Think, Rook, think.

But I don't want to think anymore. I want something to fucking work for once.

I put both of my hands on the handle, covering it completely. I know my body temp is dropping, but it is the only hope I have of the lock thawing.

Time stands still. Sound leaves me. I can't feel anything anymore. Not the lock. Not the cold. Not even my own breath.

As the darkness creeps in, I slump a little further, and the lock turns.

Chapter Sixty-Seven

Never Coming Back

Six Hazy Days Later

The smell of burning gasoline awakens me. I lean up on a bed in what appears to be a hospital hallway. Everything hurts so much I moan and plop back down. The lights flicker. Probably running on generators.

A white girl a few years older than me comes to my side and puts a damp cloth on my head. "You save your strength, dear. You've been through actual hell."

I try to speak, but the dryness in my mouth only allows me to croak out a word.

"Where?"

"You're in the Okpunichi County hospital. We've been without power for most of this past week, though you were just brought in a day ago. Do you remember what happened to you?"

I do, but I don't know if I want anyone else to know. If the police know who I am, I'm as good as jailed.

"I got attacked, got in a storm cellar, and used some supplies inside to stop my bleeding." I cough and the lady gives me a sip of water. "I had water and food, but at some point I lost track of time and must've lost consciousness."

"Well, you're something of a legend." The nurse fluffs my pillow and smiles. She grabs a TV remote and cuts on a VCR above the nurse's station. "This is the only VCR in the hospital, but I'm glad someone recorded this, because it is, well, you'll see."

A static-filled horizontal line dances across the video as garbled sounds become clearer. The standard news reporter, a white man in his thirties in a suit with perfect brown hair and teeth so white they could signal ships at sea, speaks.

"We have breaking news here at RWRS. The winter storm, dubbed The Southern Ice Storm '94, shut down a majority of the state of Mississippi. It has also uncovered a long history of crimes in the region. We cut to our junior reporter on the scene, Dallas Robinette. Dallas?"

The video screen cuts in two, with the news anchor on one side and a reporter in the backyard that I know way too well. The reporter has a puff of hair on his chin and is wearing a cowboyish hat with a white card that reads *Reporter* on the side of it. He holds his finger to one ear, awaiting the delayed cue from the news anchor.

"Yes, thank you Jamie. I am standing in the backyard of Edna Roberts, a retiree who has lived in Aichukilissa County since before its inception. Aichukilissa County, also known as "abandoned" in Chickasaw, was an area of land that was accidentally excluded from the geographical map of Mississippi for many years. Since then, its sister county Okpunichi, or the OK Punch as residents call it, has assisted in emergency and utility situations."

The video now solely focuses on the on-scene reporter. As he takes a few steps to the right, the camera follows. Yellow police tape ropes off an area behind the reporter, but I know it is the pond.

"According to Okpunichi County's sheriff, what happened at this cabin will haunt Mississippi for years to come."

A picture flashes on the screen and I'm shaken. Not because it is gruesome or shocking, but because it is a photo of me.

"Last night, Ruth Olivia Kellum, a 20-year-old African American woman from Michigan, who currently has a warrant out for her arrest, was kidnapped by Carl "Cooter" Riley, a handyman who sources say fits the exact description of the suspect behind multiple home invasions. Riley was keeping Kellum at the home of Mrs. Edna Roberts, who was also being held hostage and was apparently killed by her captor."

I am now understanding how much news anchors can distort the facts.

Dallas Robinette moves his left arm out and the camera follows him. More yellow tape and police crowd the shed in the backyard.

"Kellum, as well as the body and vehicle of highway patrolman Bobby Howler, was found today when utility workers saw what they believed to be a trail of blood going to a storm cellar. There, Kellum was found unconscious and was transported to Okpunichi County hospital. The patrolman's body was discovered in this shed, initially believed to have been killed with an ax or large knife."

The camera pans to the home and my stomach turns. I'll never look at a cabin the same way.

"Unfortunately, it appears that Carolton "Sheriff" Roberts, Jr. died while trying to save Kellum and his own mother from Riley. Some of you may remember "Sheriff" from his high school football days as an All-State quarterback. This reporter still remembers watching Sheriff throw for four touchdowns against St. Joe and how he almost won State with his teammate Stalin "Battleship" House. And, even though Sheriff was never officially part of any police organization, he was a volunteer firefighter. Flags in the county and surrounding ones will fly at half-mast today in his honor and that of Patrolman Howler."

The rage that fills me could overflow a desert. I'm the victim in this? And the *sheriff* is a freaking hero?!

Dallas Robinette walks to the right, then slips and crashes to the ground. The camera follows him as he stumbles to stand on the ice and eats it again. He tosses off his hat, revealing a balding spot in the back of his giant white head.

"You know what? (Bleep) this. (Bleep) this weather. (Bleep) this storm. (Bleep) this station. I'm done. I quit. I'm going to print news." The reporter dusts himself off and returns to split screen with the news studio. "And (Bleep) your warm (Bleep)-ing (Bleep) in the (Bleep)-ing studio, Jamie. Back to you in the (Bleep)-ing warm studio, (Bleep) hole."

At this point, all the staff and patients in the hall are watching the video, too. Even though this is a tragic story, they are laughing. The only takeaway from my night of terror. The shocked look on the news anchor's face is priceless, I must admit. It's like he swallowed some spoiled milk and was waiting to see if he would throw up or not. The pasty white anchor has gone translucent as he dabs his head with a handkerchief.

"Um, okay, well..." From off-screen, a handful of papers get handed to the anchor. He clears his throat and shuffles through them. "Thank you, Dallas. We at RWRS wish you well in your future endeavors. Ah, um, yes, in other news, it appears that the crime spree of Carl "Cooter" Riley has ended as a robbery gone wrong at *Stalin's Bar*. Paramedics got a 911 call from the establishment and arrived to find its owner,

Stalin House, wounded and Riley dead from an apparent self-inflicted gunshot to the head. More as the story unfolds and DNA results from Jackson come in."

The TV goes blank as the nurse cuts it off.

"You're so lucky that Sheriff saved you from drowning. God bless him! Oh, and of course, you."

I choke back the bile in my throat as a tremor courses through my body.

"Bless your heart, too," I muster weakly.

The nurse smiles and heads off.

As I lay in my anger, a hand touches my shoulder.

"What the hell now?" As I lean up, I'm greeted by the face of the dead. "Jesus Christ!"

"Our Lord and Savior," Stalin responds, his bushy beard unable to hide his wide smile.

I hug him and he moans.

"Careful on the gut…it's been through a lot. So, how's your week been so far?"

And with that, we both laugh, holding our various injuries.

"How come you never told me that Sheriff was a nickname, not his job?" I ask.

"Honey…" Stalin chuckles. "This is the Delta. Everyone has a nickname. Hell, even you. I just assumed you knew."

"But his radio…"

"Once a volunteer fireman, always a volunteer fireman."

"But the gun and badge…"

"Everyone carries here. And his badge was about as real as his authority. It's an antique from back when his grandfather was sheriff of Yoconna or Yokna County or something."

"He said he was going to call in my license."

"He would've," counters Stalin, "but it would've amounted to me calling it in. Concerned citizen and all that."

Before he continues, I remember the contents of Mr. Bug's trunk.

"Stalin, I found something in the trunk of Ms. Roberts' car: a box of green eyes. She was a serial killer. And—"

Stalin puts his finger over my mouth and shushes me. "I know."

"How do you know?"

"Because I found them in the trunk when I went outside to check on the phone line. I saw the trunk was open, saw the box, and found something else."

"What?"

His jaw pops as he grinds his teeth. "Validation." From his pocket, he withdraws one of the small jars with a green eye in it.

"Oh, I don't want to look at those ever again, Stalin."

"I understand, but look closely at this one."

Stalin has never steered me wrong, so I look at the eye. In the white part of the eye is a black smudge.

"What is that? An infection or something?"

"It's a birthmark." Stalin lets out a long sigh. "Just like my mother had."

I would love to say that this bit of truth, this discovery, brought closure. However, in the pain on Stalin's face, the tightness of his cheeks and tears in his eyes, this moment is anything but light.

"I am so sorry, Stalin."

Stalin wipes his left eye, then his right, before saying anything. "I, ehm, always thought I wanted to know what happened to her and, now that I do, I just, I just don't..."

I put my arms around him as much as I can. The dam bursts. I can't tell how many years of confusion, pain, doubt, and every other horrible feeling come through. But, in that moment, a man the size of a mountain crumples back into that little boy who lost his mother.

The lights in the hospital flicker, then cut off. Nurses shuffle from patient to patient, making sure everyone is okay.

The lights turn back on, and Stalin's bloodshot eyes meet mine.

"The news crew and someone from our neighboring county must've made up this story because the truth was too damaging."

"Who would've done that?" I ask.

"Someone with a lot to lose if the truth got out." He scratches his beard and shrugs. "No matter how the Powers-That-Be edit this story to fit their narrative, you and I will always know the truth."

"Well, I'm just glad—"

"Ms. Kellum?" I don't even need to see anything official to know I'm caught. The voice's question was flat, almost rhetorical. An obligation. I nod as the tall man with a crew cut holds out his badge.

"I'm U.S. Marshal David. I'm here to escort you back to Michigan."

I don't even run a Sit-Rep. There's no way out of here. I lean up and nod.

"Please rise to your feet, miss." From behind his back, Marshal David grabs silver handcuffs.

Stalin steps between the two of us. "Do you have to cuff her?"

"Standard procedure, sir."

"Stalin, it's okay." My hand on the giant's shoulder probably feels like a flea on an elephant. Still, I give him a squeeze. "I knew this was coming."

"Turn around, miss."

I can't tell what hurts more, the cut and gashes on my hands and arms, or the stitched-up wounds in the shoulder from the buckshot. As I try not to cry out, I put my hands behind my back. Frigid metal covers each wrist. The only thing colder than the cuffs is the *click-clack* sounds they make as they bind my arms.

"Do you have any possessions?" asks the Marshal.

I laugh a little, then I laugh a lot.

"I, ah, whew, can't tell you if I have a single thing to my name, Marshal."

With his hand on my shoulder, pushing me forward, we head toward the exit.

"Hey, Rook?"

I try to turn to look back, but the marshal keeps me moving forward.

"Hey, sir, just one thing before you go?"

The marshal sighs, curses, and stops our march.

I turn back to face Stalin.

"Whatever happens," he says, spreading his arms wide, "I will help you. And who knows, maybe when you're done with all this, you'll need a job."

"You're boating the wrong way, Battleship." I shake my head as the marshal grabs my shoulder and we exit the building. "I'm never coming back here."

Chapter Sixty-Eight

Epilogue: One Icy Night

Six Months Later

"Another Miller High Life, miss?" asks the guy with a full-on black mullet and a T-shirt that reads *Delta State University* and features something that looks like an angry Okra with boxing gloves.

"Champagne of Beers coming right up," I respond.

It's a hot-as-hell summer here in Mississippi. Stalin has me doing the job that Dante did, though I bet he's not concerned about me trying to rob him. After that one icy night, it turns out Dante up and joined a cult. But that's only worked out well for me. Now that I'm officially twenty-one, I can tend bar AND drink. Hell, Stalin liked me so much he gave me a set of keys to the bar. I sleep on the cot up top. It's not glamorous, but it's a start.

And I've got good ole Cotton to cuddle at night.

With the money from his mother's life insurance policy, Stalin not only fixed up this bar; he got me the best lawyer in Michigan well-versed in patients' rights. I'd love to say that my case was solid. It wasn't. I was as guilty as a kid with a hand in the cookie jar.

But I had a lawyer that was connected. The lawyer was also a cousin to the presiding judge, through marriage, not blood.

Conflicts of interest be damned. Nepotism and cold hard cash got me probation for my identify theft and fraud charges. My lawyer made a case about how we would willingly go to a jury trial, especially since the news of my surviving the famous ice storm went national. It also helped my case that the agents in the hospital brought a convicted felon into my gramma's room, cuffed me to a bed, and left me and her in an unsafe situation. *Illegal, inhumane, and unnecessary detainment,* said my lawyer. And it really helped that my name is about as synonymous with this new storm as Baby Jessica.

I whip out a bottle opener from my back pocket and pop open the beer, and Stalin enters his establishment to cheers.

"Thank you, you bunch of heathens!"

Everyone laughs as patrons shake his hand and pat him on the back.

"For everyone that needs to know, my asshole works again!"

More laughs and cheers fill the tin building. I hang my head; there are less-crude ways to announce the removal of the colostomy bag and the reattaching of Stalin's insides.

Stalin really came through for me, and not just with the lawyer. He gave me the money to buy my next vehicle: Mr. Bug.

That's right; I bought the clunker at a police auction for about three hundred bucks. At least now, I'll never be without wheels.

I can't say why, but I glance at Riley's yellow raincoat still on the coatrack. Neither Stalin nor I can bring ourselves to get rid of it. A bittersweet reminder of how close each of us came to being on the wrong side of the grass.

By the time the big man gets to me, I've already got the jug on the bar.

Stalin smiles and rotates the *Entrepierna Del Diablo* in his mitt as I slide two empty shot glasses his way. Stalin pours each of us a shot and raises his glass in a toast.

It's our own personal drinkable badge of honor.

"To being warriors."

I repeat it, and we clink.

"It's not...that bad..." I choke out over the liquor.

"Like hell it's not..." Stalin coughs and laughs, coughing all the harder.

"It's...kinda...minty..." I try.

"It's *kinda minty* like a foot in an ass. Then someone ground up that foot and put it into a bottle of shitty tequila."

"I said *kinda*."

We laugh as someone drags Stalin away. As I look around this shitty bar in the middle of nowhere, I can't help but smile.

I'm excited to see what future adventures this part of the world has in store for me.

THE END

This FREE W.A. Pepper Technothriller is Available Now at http://tanto-dogoodr.wapepperwrites.com/

Tanto and his team of hackers must beat a ticking clock to save a stranger from a lifetime jail sentence. How far will Tanto risk his own freedom to protect a kid who made a mistake? To read the first chapter, please continue reading. To read the first chapter, please turn the page.

My Damn Life

Abort.

That's what my gut tells me as I walk headlong towards the cop that's tailed me for the last two blocks.

In one hand, I have a cup of coffee. In the other, a magazine. While nothing is technically in his hands, his right hand rests on his service weapon.

My gut also told me *abort* yesterday when the most emo hacker I've ever worked with messaged me about meeting with a client about a job. During the whole nine-hour bus ride here, my brain and my instincts wrestled with each other. My brain very rightly pointed out that going after such a high-level government agency would put me on their radar. For over half a decade, I've flown under it, so why would I dare rock the boat now? That's easy, countered my gut, reminding me of the last thing written in the post, the nail in my decision coffin:

For DJ.

Even though my gut is currently winning the battle of wills, my brain isn't wrong: everything about this gig* points to failure. For the past couple of hours, I've walked all over this subdivision of Miami, Florida, overhearing pedestrians complaining about everything from finding a parking place to the overbearing heat.

And, somewhere along the way, I earned a beat cop as a tail. No one is as pissed off as beat cops. They're the guys who don't have an air-conditioned squad car and are just looking for any excuse to pat down or bust someone. Sometimes they are police that are starting out, but judging from the age of this guy, he messed up and got bumped down to grunt work.

When you also factor in the blazing heat and this sketchy black hoodie that makes me sweat like a whore in church, I haven't done myself any favors. However, if I break my stride, I'll throw any chance I have of getting rid of him.

Sweat drips from my palms to the magazine. My fingers itch from the perspiration. Unfortunately, I'll need to put down my coffee cup in order to pull this off. I just hope that my sudden shift isn't enough to be classified what the po-po call a *potentially aggressive movement*: anything that is a sudden change from a normal stance or situation.

I approach a standard blue mailbox, the kind you find on every other street corner, while still facing the officer. I might as well be an extrovert because I go so far against my self-preservation.

"Oh, thank goodness you're here, officer!" I yell, putting my coffee cup on top of the mailbox. He's not buying my act, because now his non-gun hand has moved to the radio transmitter on the left side of his neck. One squawk from that and any anonymity I have is gone.

From the inside of the magazine, I grab my map. It's not just any map; it is a tourist map. You know the kind, the one that folds up to the size of an envelope and, when you unfold it, there are ads for every money-grubbing tourist trap out there.

Even from five feet away, the officer's full body sigh has hurricane-level winds.

He probably would rather shoot me than help me guess where to find Gloria Estefan's star on the Latin Walk of Fame. That's part of the *serve* in *protect and serve*, I guess.

"Oh, sorry," he says as he squawks his own radio. "Have to take this. Go ahead, Dispatch. Over."

As he hurries away, I hear *Dispatch* answer, "Negative. That wasn't on our end. Over."

It isn't until the cop is completely out of sight that I realize my full body shakes like I am standing in a freezer. This gig hasn't even officially started, and I'm already so full of bile that I'm practically a Bourbon Street

gutter. It's more than the encounter with the cop. I'm risking every-thing – from my freedom to my life – for someone I'll never meet.

And I'm doing it because I was just that age when someone stuck their neck out for this stranger and saved my damn life.

Continued in the FREE ebook at http://tanto-dogoodr.wapepp erwrites.com/

Afterword – The Delta Ice Storm, 30 Years Later

Sudden events mark, if not mar, our lives. Some focus on achievements or prosperity. Others, failures, or losses. And then there are the ones that start in tragedy and end in triumph.

Thirty years ago, there was a storm that redefined the way I live. Growing up, the main moments that stuck out to me were the Challenge Explosion and the fall of the Berlin Wall. But those events weren't in my backyard. The 1994 Delta Ice Storm hit during my freshman year in high school. Growing up in the small Mississippi Delta town of Cleveland, we saw the occasional snow. I'd seen a good bit of ice and snow before, mainly when my family went to Colorado.

But nothing like this.

Even though it was February, we should've known something bad was on the way because the temperature hit 70 degrees. Then it plummeted to 28 degrees as a cold front mixed with that warm front.

My parents' house had a bunch of trees that they'd planted when they built that house. Throughout the night, sounds like small arms gunfire popped as limb after limb struggled to handle the 3X to 4X their weight in ice. Thunderous crashes echoed through our home as trees toppled. Finally, the booms of power lines crashing and their transformers exploding added to the chaos.

350,000 people went without power for an average of 7 days, and that was just in Mississippi. Almost 26 thousand power line poles covered our yards and streets. At the time, this was the largest and costliest disaster in Mississippi Power & Light history. The damage to the southern part of the United States was in the billions. Alabama and Tennessee each had damage reaching over half a billion. Mississippi wasn't as lucky, where the damage and loss of revenue reached over two billion.

For the next three weeks, my parents and I went without power and, sometimes, water. You'd think I'd look back on that time with fear or boredom. Instead, I remember all the wonderful experiences that came out of the storm. With houses losing heat, you'd think everyone would've stayed to themselves. Instead, the kindness of a community coming together shined more brightly than the sun off the icy snow. People grabbed their gear to help move downed trees, share supplies, and cook meals. I remember my dad and I cooked catfish and hushpuppies for all the power line and rescue workers at our local Moose Lodge. It was my first time cooking hushpuppies, and I still smile when I think about those balls of batter crackling and watching them turn from light brown to dark.

But it wasn't all fun and cooking hushpuppies. I had a friend and classmate who lost his father during this time. The kind man was trying to help others, and a fall took his life. I remember attending that funeral in a mostly dark hall, and wearing a heavy coat since the heat was out.

As I said at the beginning, this event changed the way I live. I learned poker from friends as we huddled around a table that was warmed by a portable kerosine heater. Today, my wife and I have gas heat/gas stoves because electricity can be taken away by a storm. We keep bottled water, batteries, canned goods, and more on hand at all times. We fill the bathtubs when a storm comes through, just in case we lose water. And so many other things that changed our daily lives.

Thank you for reading our book, One Icy Night: A Rook Thriller. This story allowed me to revisit this impactful time in my life. I hope you, the reader, felt its power in these pages. Be well and keep hustling wisely, Will

Special Thanks

There are three ways to ultimate success: The first way is to be kind. The second way is to be kind. The third way is to be kind. – Mr. Rogers

It's probably weird that I would write about kindness at the end of a suspenseful thriller. However, without kindness, this book wouldn't exist.

I believe a kind and all-powerful being granted me the opportunity to not only write, but to share my writing. I know that God put me on this earth to tell stories that have kindness in them. For this, I am thankful.

Every single day, my wife Taddy is kind and supportive of my writing. Even when I disagree with her (always correct) feedback, she delivers it in a kind fashion. I know I can be difficult taking advice, especially from a loved one, but this book shines because Taddy expects, no, demands great stories. Thank you, Babe.

In addition, I would like to thank the following people who contributed to this work currently in your hands:

Developmental Editor Meaghan Wagner took up this thriller and hit me with story-encouraging feedback. Our cover artist Damon Freeman and his team asked what I saw on the cover, and they made it a reality. Finally, David Sandretto's always excellent eye for details caught many a mistake as our copyeditor/proofreader. Thank you to this amazing team.

Our team of Beta Readers pointed out details and insights and offer suggestions that I never would've caught on my own. A big thank you to Cathy T., Josi D. (VW bug operating), Kenneth M., Mike I.C. (medical), Margery T., and Richard D.

I would also like to thank our friend Hadonica M., who not only let me ask what I call my DWB (dumb white boy) questions (how do you take care of dreds, what do scars look like on black skin, etc.), but was extremely kind and helpful with her answers.

Authors I would like to thank include (in alphabetical order): Taylor Adams, Tara Alemany, Lee Child, Shawn Coyne, Rachel Hawkins, Mark Leslie Lefebvre (who helped with the title and influential reading), Kiersten Modglin, Riley Sager, Kevin Smith, Ruth Ware, and Andrew Van Wey.

Others I would like to thank include (in alphabetical order): Dan Alexander, Iman Benson, Brian Bosworth, Ben Brower, Bruce Butler, Pam Burleson, Rex Davis, Viola Davis, Lisa Emery, Scott Frank, Rachel Hawkins, Tom Pelphrey, Brian O'Halloran, Will Rogers, Octavia Spencer, Cicely Tyson, K. Trevor Wilson,

And to everyone who supports W.A. Pepper Writes, and Hustle Valley Press, LLC.

Thank you all!

About the Author

W. A. Pepper puts lies on paper. His wife puts them in books that people can buy, borrow, or steal. Technically, he writes suspenseful thrillers. *You Will Know Vengeance* was his debut novel. While it won over ten book awards, it did lose the Pulitzer Prize. He is an awarding-winning *USA Today*, *Wall Street Journal*, and *Amazon* Bestselling Author for his contribution to the business anthology *Habits of Success*. He has a PhD in Management Information Systems or, as he calls it, Business Computing, from The University of Mississippi. Finally, he, his wife Taddy, and their dog Danger split their time between Colorado and Mississippi.

CONTACT INFORMATION

- will@hustlevalleypress.com

- Instagram:@wapepperwrites

- Facebook.com/wapepperwrites

- Tiktok.com/@wapepperwrites